RHONE

Former bounty hunter Phil Rhone finds himself in a mess of trouble when he agrees to help Brad Miller to find his abducted wife, Lorna. They team up with Susan Prescott, a blonde beauty seeking the killers of her family. The hunt takes them up into the isolated mountains to a slave labour gold mine, where they confront sadistic Nelson Forbes. The odds are against them, but Susan thirsts for revenge and Miller isn't leaving without his wife . . .

*Books by James Gordon White
in the Linford Western Library:*

COMMANCHE CAPTIVE

JAMES GORDON WHITE

RHONE

Complete and Unabridged

LINFORD
Leicester

First published in Great Britain in 1996 by
Robert Hale Limited
London

First Linford Edition
published 1999
by arrangement with
Robert Hale Limited
London

British Library CIP Data

White, James Gordon
  Rhone.—Large print ed.—
  Linford western library
  1. Western stories
  2. Large type books
  I. Title
  823.9′14 [F]

  ISBN 0–7089–5429–4

Published by
F. A. Thorpe (Publishing) Ltd.
Anstey, Leicestershire

Set by Words & Graphics Ltd.
Anstey, Leicestershire
Printed and bound in Great Britain by
T. J. International Ltd., Padstow, Cornwall

This book is printed on acid-free paper

To
Marie, James Sr. and Solveig

1

Brad Miller was lost.

Hopelessly and absolutely lost.

Was he going in circles, or was the damn desert never-changing? The paloverdes, pipe organ cactus and stunted mesquite trees all looked the same as those he had been passing since dawn. The mountains, which had first seemed so near, continued to remain elusive, taunting his progress. It was still early morning but the sun, bearing down out of a cloudless, yellow-tinged sky, warned of the heat and misery soon to come.

Brad scowled and waved irritably at the gnats buzzing his face as he studied the broken, baked land ahead. The aggressive insects were not the least intimidated and kept trying to fly up his nose and into his panting mouth. Keeping a wary watch for rattlesnakes that might be sunning themselves around rocks, he began walking.

For about the hundredth time this morning he cursed his impatience in not waiting a week for the delayed stagecoach. Sure Lorna had been in favour of his decision, but they should have stayed in Dry Fork. Though dull and boring, the one-horse town had at least been relatively safe. Now Lorna had been abducted to God knows where, and he was stumbling around in the desert trying to find her. Not being a frontiersman, there was a very real possibility that he might well die a merciless, long, drawn out death in this wilderness and never be found.

Brad quickly forced the morbid thought from his mind before it brought crippling panic and despair. If he surrendered, both he and Lorna were lost. He concentrated on letting her image fill his mind's eye. He saw Lorna's beautiful oval face, framed by thick, straight red hair that complemented her smooth ivory skin. Slanting brows and long dark lashes accentuated her seductive green eyes. Smiling red lips and a tilted nose completed her delicately moulded features. She was less than medium height, which suited Brad, who was only slightly over that himself. Her figure was slender, full-bosomed and narrow-waisted. Brad smiled and continued to think about his bride of two weeks.

Lorna seemed so much wiser and worldlier at twenty-one than he did at twenty-six. He attributed it to having grown up in a solid, middle-class atmosphere, while he had been raised with all the privileges of wealth, not to mention an overbearing father who had unwittingly instilled doubt and insecurity in him about his own worth. Brad did not consider himself a weakling; still, he was a far cry from the swaggering cowboys he had seen during his travels. Going straight from Harvard into his father's banking firm also had not helped his self-confidence.

He constantly felt that he was having to prove himself to everyone there, especially his father.

A loud, high-pitched rattling burst in on Brad's thoughts and halted him in mid-stride. About three feet in front of him a large prairie rattler was coiling to strike. It had blended in with its surroundings and he had not seen the snake until he was almost on top of it.

Beady eyes radiant with malice, curved fangs gleaming wickedly in its wide mouth, the serpent raised its ugly head and faced the intruder.

Brad stood stock-still. He did not know whether all the stories he had heard about their deadliness were true, or merely tall tales spun at the expense of gullible Easterners, but a rattlesnake bite was the last thing he needed. Weaponless, his only defence would be a mad dash.

Rattles rapidly buzzing while its hissing, forked tongue flicked in and out between its twin fangs, the snake pulled back its head and then struck.

Brad leaped aside as the ugly head shot forward, its sharp, erected fangs protruding ahead of its upper jaw. The lunge fell short. Before the snake could position itself for another strike Brad whirled and took to his heels.

Only when he was a safe distance away did he stop and stand catching his breath. He had survived his first (and hopefully last) encounter with a rattlesnake. It had been a very ignominious experience, but again 'discretion was the better part of valour'.

Looking about at the harsh expanse, Brad again cursed his decision to travel on to another town and catch a connecting stagecoach. Will Craddock, their guide, had assured them that there was no danger from outlaws or Indians. Of course not, the danger had been from him and his brawny half-breed helper. Brad should have been suspicious of Craddock's rugged, seedy appearance, but then one expected the inhabitants of a frontier outpost to be colourful. Lorna had suffered terribly from motion sickness, due to the constant rocking in every direction of the suspended coach in its low-slung leather braces, and the thought of escaping such torment for a few days had been heaven. Besides, she had understood his anxiety to reach San Francisco and take over his new position in his father's banking branch there. It represented a new life and a chance to finally stand on his own two feet.

Brad smiled, remembering Lorna's apprehension on seeing the saddled horses and being informed that there was not a sidesaddle to be found in over five hundred miles. Though her riding habit was more suited for a park than the rugged West Lorna had gamely made do with both it and a man's saddle without complaint.

Things had gone well the first day. He and Lorna had been more than a little saddle sore that night, but

Craddock had assured them it was to be expected. Camping out had been an exhilarating experience; he had never seen so many stars in the sky before. The next morning they had broken camp at the first light of dawn and travelled until the heat of day forced them to halt for several hours. Brad had come to expect men admiring Lorna so he had not thought much about Craddock's sly glances toward her throughout the day. He should have.

That night, minds on reaching civilisation the following day, he and Lorna had ignored Craddock and his helper talking in low tones on the far side of camp and wearily rolled into their blankets. Sometime near morning Brad had been awakened by sounds of a struggle and Lorna's muffled cry. Groggily sitting up, he had seen Lorna, one long ivory leg kicking free of her blanket, writhing in Craddock's grasp. Then he'd heard movement behind him and his brain had suddenly exploded in a blinding, violent pain as Craddock's helper slugged him with something very hard.

He had regained consciousness with a fierce headache at false dawn. Stumbling to his feet, he had found himself alone in an empty camp with his and Lorna's belongings strewn about, her boots and jacket still beside her rumpled blanket. After grimly assessing his situation he had begun following the hoofprints deeper into the desert until they were finally lost.

Brad abruptly came out of his reverie with a heart-twisting jerk at the distant, but fast approaching sound of hoofbeats. He scrambled up a small rise and stared toward another area of the distant mountains.

Dust swirling behind, a lone horseman was galloping hell for leather away from the mountains.

Brad shouted hoarsely and jumped about flapping his arms like a scarecrow in a wind storm. The rider saw him, slowed, then veered in his direction.

Brad continued waving until the dark shapeless form slowly took on the separate, distinct figures of man and horse, then staggered down the rise to meet his rescuer. He was aware of the chance he was taking, the stranger might be a desperado. Well, there was nothing for him to take but his life, and the desert might claim that anyway before the day was out. Breath tight in his chest, Brad stood watching as the horseman reined up before him.

The tall man looked down from his tall horse. His long, tanned, weathered face hinted dismay as his brown eyes ranged over Brad's dishevelled appearance. The fancy ruffled shirt, expensive cut dark pants, spats and bowler derby were in sharp contrast to the stranger's faded, simple clothing. Denims, blue work shirt, yellow kerchief, scuffed boots and a battered black, low-crowned hat with a wide, curving brim all seemed at home on the stranger's lanky frame, as did the cartridge belt and holstered Colt .44.

'I'd say maybe you're kinda lost,' the stranger remarked dryly, his soft drawl immediately establishing him as a Southerner.

Brad hesitated, aware that his thick Boston accent would betray him as a 'damnyankee'. Though the war had been over for three years there were still those in both the North and South who nursed animosities — and Southern pride bitterly resented the repressive Reconstruction that had been forced upon the defeated South. He couldn't remain mute for ever, not if he wanted the man's help. 'Yes,' he replied. 'I was left stranded.'

'Yankee, huh?' the man commented matter-of-factly, his ruggedly handsome features reflecting no bitterness. Brad was also relieved that he had not prefaced the word with 'damn'.

'Boston.'

'Figured some place like that,' the tall man said, and cast a wary glance back over a broad shoulder at the mountains.

'I need help,' Brad said urgently.

The stranger turned back to him and frowned thoughtfully. 'I don't know as I'm the man you want.'

'What do you mean?' Brad asked incredulously.

'You see, right now I'm bein' hunted.'

'You're an outlaw?' Brad asked, his hopes sinking.

'No. But there's a pack of 'em after me.' He jerked a thumb back at the mountains. 'Delayed 'em some by blockin' the trail. Sooner or later they'll find another one and come boilin' down offa that mountain. Got a pretty fair lead now, carryin' double will cut it in half.'

'How do you know they will keep following you?'

'Bob Templeton won't quit till he's dead. Seems I killed his younger brother down on the Gila River about two years ago.' He smiled at Brad's surprise and added, 'I was bounty huntin' at the time, and Mort Templeton elected

11

to fight instead of comin' along peaceably.' He shrugged. 'Ol' Mort never was too bright.'

'Then it was self-defence,' Brad said, somewhat relieved.

The tall man nodded. 'But that don't matter none to Bob.' He eyed Brad evenly. 'Now that you know where you stand, you still wantta come along?'

'Absolutely,' Brad answered without hesitation; a possible death by outlaws was preferable to a certain one alone in the desert.

'Reckon you'd best at that,' the tall man agreed. 'Bob and his boys will shoot you outta pure meanness if they come across you out here.' He leaned down and extended an arm.

Catching the man's arm, Brad awkwardly swung up behind him. As he settled himself behind the cantle he noticed what appeared to be sand trickling from several bullet holes in a saddlebag pouch. 'Say, did you know . . . ' he began curiously.

'Save it,' the tall man interrupted

curtly. 'We got some hard ridin' to do.' With that he jabbed his heels into the sorrel's flanks. Brad frantically grabbed the man's waist as the big gelding lunged forward.

★ ★ ★

An hour later found the two men resting in the shade around a small waterhole. Like most Easterners Brad had imagined a pristine Sahara oasis, and he had first been appalled by the various feathers floating on the clear water and the droppings and other waste left at the edge or in the water by four-footed creatures. But faced with the even more unpleasant alternative of dying of thirst, he had put aside prejudice and drank as heartily as his companion.

Squinting against the bright sunlight, Brad finished his tale of Lorna's abduction while the tall man, who had introduced himself as Phil Rhone, refilled his empty canteen.

'They most likely took her to Free Town,' Rhone said, sitting back and recapping the canteen.

'Isn't that risky?' Brad asked. 'Surely the authorities would hear about Lorna?'

'Free Town is an old gold town that was abandoned years ago, after the strike played out. Now it's a place where outlaws meet and trade. Nobody in his right mind goes there.'

'Will you guide me to it?'

'You want to commit suicide just stay right here and wait for Bob Templeton and his gang.'

'You don't have to go into the town. Just take me there.'

'I got healthier things to do. Besides, even if I was of a mind to, how in hell are you gonna rescue her?'

'I'll think of something.'

'Were you in the late War?'

'No.'

'Ever shot a weapon before?'

'No.' Rhone let his breath out in a long oral sigh. Brad quickly continued before he could speak. 'But I am mad enough to kill those bastards for what they have done.'

'I don't blame you,' Rhone agreed sympathetically. 'Still, it's no job for a Boston, Massachusetts banker.'

'If you are offering your services,' Brad said hopefully, 'I will be glad to pay.'

'Keep your money.' Rhone grinned and pointed to his horse, standing in the shade of a large rock. 'I got enough gold in my saddlebags so that I don't have to risk my life.'

Brad gaped in surprise as he suddenly realised that it had been gold dust instead of sand trickling out of the pouch. Well, Rhone's loss might just be his gain. 'You had better check your saddlebags,' he said casually.

Rhone scowled, carried the canteen to the horse and slung it over the pommel Then he saw the bullet holes in the saddlebag and, his concern building, urgently tore open the pouch. Of the six sacks inside only one small sack partly retained its contents; the rest were torn open and empty. Rhone quickly turned to Brad and angrily demanded, 'Why didn't you tell me before now?'

'I tried to,' Brad said innocently, secretly relishing Rhone's distress. 'But you told me to save it because we had a hard ride ahead of us.'

'That's no excuse,' Rhone roared.

'I didn't know what it was. I have never seen gold dust before. I thought it was sand.'

'Expensive goddamn sand!' Rhone took out the small sack and weighed it in his palm. 'More'n a year spent pannin' in freezin' mountain streams — and this is all I have to show for it!'

Brad could not work up much sympathy, his mind was on Free Town and Lorna's rescue. He waited until Rhone's rage changed to despair and then made his pitch. 'Look, my family is rich. I will pay you a thousand dollars to help me find Lorna.'

Rhone looked up from carefully

scraping the loose dust into the small sack. 'You realise we could both be killed.'

'Lorna is worth that risk,' Brad said sincerely.

'Not to me,' Rhone said flatly.

'Twenty-five hundred dollars then,' Brad said, his grey eyes steely with purpose.

Rhone considered. Maybe fate was trying to make up for his loss by throwing him together with this tenderfoot. He sure did not look forward to another year of panning for gold. He was being offered a quick way out — provided he didn't get killed. He appraised Bradley K. Miller, Jr. closely.

He was medium height and build. His cultured Boston accent, reserved manner and aristocratic features all said that he had not known a day of deprivation. Rhone felt more than a twinge of envy and resentment. Born thirty-three years ago in the Big Thicket area of east Texas, about three million acres of oak and pine forests, scattered swamps and black-water sloughs, he had grown up hard, scrapping to live. He had serious doubts about the capabilities of the softly handsome young man before him who, despite his money, projected an air of insecurity. Common sense told him to forget it and ride away. Greed told him to stay. Greed won out.

'All right, I want five thousand dollars,' Rhone said firmly. If he was going to risk his life it was going to be worthwhile. That money would ensure starting his long-dreamed-of ranch.

'Done,' Brad said eagerly. He stood and strode to Rhone. They sealed the bargain with a handshake, and he winced inwardly at Rhone's strong grip. Restraining the urge to wring his smarting hand, he asked, 'Now which way is Free Town?'

Rhone shook his head. 'We hafta make another stop first.'

'Why?' Brad asked, frowning impatiently.

Rhone motioned back the way they had come. 'Bob Templeton and his men.'

'Couldn't we just try to lose them?'

Rhone shook his head. 'Not ridin' double.' He saw Brad's disappointment. 'There's no other way. We're gonna have to fight 'em and I'd rather pick the spot.' He squinted up at the sun. 'There's a ghost town not too far from here. We'll make our stand there.'

'Suppose we get killed?'

Rhone shrugged his broad shoulders. 'Then I'm out five thousand dollars.' He grinned reassuringly. 'Don't fret, I plan to make damn sure that won't happen.'

As Brad again mounted behind Rhone he tried to tell himself that things were now promising, but all he could think about was the upcoming battle with a band of outlaws.

The thought was more than a little unsettling.

2

The man known only as Sardo rode into the broad, mountain-ringed valley at the head of three hardcases. Tall, muscularly lean, hawk-faced, hair prematurely salt and pepper, Sardo rode ramrod straight, with a military bearing. Ten of his thirty-five years had indeed been spent in the Cavalry, until he had found it was much more profitable to hire out his services to the highest bidder. As a result, his body bore a multitude of scars, and he had lost his left eye in a range war down in Texas. Since then he had worn a black patch distinctly decorated with a large blood-shot eye, which was unsettling to both friends and enemies alike. For the past two years he had been comfortably employed as mine owner Nelson Forbes' top gun, and was returning from carrying out just such a chore. Killing always put him in a good mood for days.

Turning his big bay towards the road leading to Forbes' sprawling house, Sardo left the three men to continue on to the guards' quarters a half-mile ahead. The two-storey house, with its yawning, immaculate grounds, was befitting of royalty, and Nelson Forbes was the undisputed king of this vast section of lower Colorado.

A guard armed with a big, long-barrelled Sharps rifle recognised Sardo's black-clad figure and waved as he rode up and halted before the wide veranda of the plantation style house. They exchanged greetings, then before Sardo could step down the man said, 'Mister Forbes is at the pit.'

'What's the occasion?' Sardo asked, settling back into his saddle.

'Whilst you was gone some workmen escaped. Led us on a good chase 'fore they was finally caught.' The man paused to spit into the flower bed and shift his wad of tobacco to the other cheek. 'One is still missin'. Reckoned to have fell off a mountainside.' He grinned and jerked a thumb toward the back of the house. 'If'n you hurry you might git there 'fore the fun's over.' Sardo nodded and turned his bay toward a corner of the house. The guard stared after him and, despite Nelson Forbes' standing order, sent another stream of brown tobacco juice into the multicoloured flower bed.

Careful to keep the bay out of the back yard, with its flowers, shrubs and hanging Japanese lanterns, Sardo rode past the servants' quarters and was nearing the stable and corral when distant excited, cheering voices reached him. He continued following the voices toward a pit near the base of a mountain where the human blood-sports were being held.

Damn, he hoped he would not arrive too late.

* * *

A pickaxe *swooshed* down in a deadly arc and rang metallically against the side of a blocking pickaxe. The attacker nimbly danced away, and the two men once more began cautiously circling and feinting. The shrieking men and women clustered around the sides of the wide, ten-foot deep pit eagerly wagered back and forth and demanded death for the sweaty, bare-chested contestants below.

Seated in a high-back wooden chair at one end of the pit, Nelson Forbes ignored the champagne sloshing from his crystal glass onto his white silk shirt and black pants and maniacally howled right along with the others.

Tall, lean, black hair greying at the temples, Forbes' sculptured features and cultured Southern manners made him appear quite out of place in the company of coarse gunmen and their equally coarse trollops. Like his Virginia forebears, Forbes had carved out his own empire built and maintained by slave labour. Indians, fugitives, gold-seekers and other adventurers who strayed into his domain were hunted down and enslaved. Law was non-existent in the vast areas between the scattered frontier settlements, and the few lawmen who ever ventured into Forbes' domain were content to look the other way, as his generosity more than adequately supplemented their meagre monthly salaries.

'*Mi amor*, your *gringo* is doing badly against my *hombre*,' purred Rosa, his current mistress.

Forbes scowled over at the shapely Mexican beauty seated beside him, heavy, pitch-black hair framing her brown, high-cheekboned face. 'A city criminal is more cunning than an ignorant *peon*, my dear,' he replied confidently.

Rosa's black eyebrows arched over her challenging dark eyes. 'You would care to wager another twenty dollars, *mi amor*?'

'Two hundred,' shrugged Forbes.

The point of Rosa's tongue crept out

and licked thoughtfully at her full, ripe lips as she watched the contest below. Then she sighed, her firm bosom thrusting against the thin material of her peasant blouse, and purred, 'Very well, if you wish to throw your money away?'

'It is you who are throwing your money away,' Forbes gloated.

'No, Nelson,' Rosa said in a sultry tone. 'I shall be rich.' She laughed in her throat, took a sip of champagne and eyed him mockingly over the rim of her glass.

The rapid tattoo of ringing steel drew their eyes back to the combatants. The criminal from St. Louis was retreating from the Mexican *peon*'s fierce attack. Both cheering their own man, Forbes and Rosa leaned forward in their chairs as the battle moved toward them. The Mexican was beginning to tire, the strength of each succeeding swing was not as powerful as the one before. Suddenly the criminal side-stepped and swung, intent on driving his pick through his opponent's ribs. He almost accomplished his goal.

Pivoting, the Mexican put his remaining strength behind a swift, downward swing that split the man's blond head in two. The criminal fell like a pole-axed steer and lay twitching in his death-throes. The crowd erupted in howls of victory and groans of disappointment.

'Damn it to hell,' Forbes exploded, hurling his glass away and glaring down at the spasmodic body spreading its gore across the dirt.

'I won,' Rosa cried joyfully. She leaned over and threw her arms around Forbes' neck. 'Now pay me, *mi amor*!'

Shouting his rage, Forbes tore Rosa's arms from his neck, lunged to his feet, upsetting his chair, and leaped down into the pit. The crowd instantly fell silent, all eyes riveted on Forbes. Clutching his dripping pickaxe, the panting, blood-splattered Mexican watched in surprise as Forbes bent and pried the weapon from the corpse's still-quivering hands.

'Now fight me, you son of a bitch!'

The Mexican came at him without hesitation. Forbes effortlessly blocked the man's frenzied blows and then launched his own furious attack. The crowd again erupted into noise, anxiously urging Forbes on as he drove the retreating man back across the pit. Unlike his awkward opponent Forbes fought with a cold, ruthless passion. He saw, even smelled, the Mexican's fear and desperation as he was driven back, step by step, until his back was against the dirt wall. A powerful swipe tore the pick from the man's hands and sent it tumbling across the ground. The crowd became hushed, waiting expectantly for the kill.

'*Misericordia . . . por favor!*' the Mexican pleaded, his eyes on the raised pickaxe glinting in the sunlight.

Nelson Forbes was in no mood for mercy, but the sight of Sardo shoving his way to the front of the group gathered directly above him halted his killing stroke. There were now more important matters to attend to. His rage vanishing he called to Sardo, who smiled and nodded in acknowledgement, then placed the pick's sharp tip against the cowering man's bare chest and said sternly, 'The next time I bet against you, Mes-can, you better lose!' The *peon* stood motionless, not daring to breathe. Forbes savoured his fear, then casually discarded the pick and stalked toward a ladder at the far end of the pit.

Sardo was waiting by the time Forbes climbed out. 'Damn it all,' Forbes exclaimed. 'Things just seem to go to pieces whenever you are gone, Sardo.' He clapped a hand on the gunman's shoulder and led him away from the others.

'I heard about the workers' escape,' Sardo said.

'That was not all. Pa Dagget and his filthy lot raided the last gold shipment and made off with nearly ten thousand dollars!' He eyed Sardo with a wounded expression. 'Do you have any idea how it makes me feel when scum like that put something over on me?'

'You want'em dusted,' Sardo said stoically.

Forbes smiled. 'I knew you would understand.'

'Consider it done.'

'Now tell me about that other 'petty' annoyance you were to deal with for me.'

'Matt Prescott won't be writing any more letters to the Territorial authorities. Seems he and his family were massacred by 'Arapahos' a few days ago.'

'That *is* a pity,' Forbes said, looking the picture of true sorrow.

'The pity was his daughter. A beautiful young blonde.'

'I wish you had brought her back,' Forbes said, scowling over at Rosa who sat guzzling champagne from the bottle. 'Rosa is becoming so . . . tedious.'

'There might have been a search for the girl. This way it's just another small rancher and his family who got wiped out by murdering savages.' He grinned knowingly and added, 'The Cavalry is already spread too thin and has more important concerns.'

'That's what I like about you, Sardo,' Forbes said cheerfully, 'you are always thinking. Why I do believe you are almost as smart as me.'

Sardo was saved from a tactful denial by Rosa's drunken shout. 'The next two are about to fight. Do you wish to make another bet, *mi amor*?'

Forbes admirably restrained himself and wondered how it would feel to kill a woman. He must ask Sardo some time. He waved for her to be quiet and turned back to Sardo. 'After you have dealt with Pa Dagget and set a brutal example for the other outlaws in this area, stop by Free Town and see if any interesting women are being sold. You know my taste.' Sardo nodded. Forbes grinned and clapped him on the shoulder. 'Fetch me a fresh, new beauty so I can send Rosa to the whores' shacks and be rid of her.'

'If that's what you want?' Sardo said with a shrug.

'Very badly.'

'When do I leave?'

'Tomorrow morning will be soon enough.' Forbes began walking Sardo back to the pit. 'Until then relax and enjoy yourself. You have arrived in time for the last contest. I only chose four of the men who were recaptured for this little entertainment. I must not be *too* wasteful with my labourers.'

Sardo only half listened to Forbes' droning voice, his mind was already anxiously plotting his next kill.

* * *

The late morning sun scorched its way across the copper sky, thinning and exhausting the desert air. Brad Miller felt as though he was enclosed in an airless vice as he staggered over the hot ground, straggling farther and farther behind Rhone who trudged

31

along leading the weary horse. Sweat made tiny channels in the dust caking his face and stung his eyes; he had long since given up mopping his brow with his damp shirt sleeve. He was willing to bet he had sweated several gallons. His expensive ruffled shirt was a ruin of sweat and wrinkles, clinging wetly to his back and under his arms. He drew small comfort from the fact that Rhone's blue work shirt was in no better shape, its wide dark stains rimmed white with salt.

The violent, desolate beauty of his surroundings were entirely wasted as Brad, thoroughly miserable, desperately concentrated on each struggling step forward. The only sounds breaking the deathly stillness were the muffled thud of hoofs in the loose sand and the horse's laboured gasps. Of course he and Rhone were doing some gasping of their own, too. Dust rose from every step the horse took and drifted back on him, settling over his clothes, face and in his nostrils. Brad coughed and spat.

A very ungentlemanly act, but then the desert was no place for gentlemen.

How much farther was this ghost town?

In spite of the oven-hot air Brad felt a sudden chill at the thought of what would occur after they had finally reached their destination. Civilised men did not engage in Dime Novel shootouts. But this was the 'wild West' and not staid Boston. A lizard scurrying to the protection of a nearby clump of greasewood confirmed the fact and also reminded him that the desert contained all sorts of crawling species — especially rattlesnakes. He tried not to dwell on it and focused his sole attention on placing one weary foot in front of the other and continuing his forward motion.

Rhone topped a slight rise and paused, gasping along with the blowing sorrel, to see what lay ahead. Through shimmering heat waves rising from the baked earth he stared down at the weathered remains of a one-street ghost town less than half a mile away. Once again that old familiar unsettling feeling came over him.

Damn, he hated ghost towns!

It was not because of any superstitious nonsense. Desert ghost towns seemed to bring home to him the smallness and frailties of man. All man-made structures existed upon the sufferage of the desert, and once abandoned, the desert swiftly returned to take up its former claim. It made him feel pretty insignificant in the scheme of things to know that through wind, heat and sudden floods the desert would finally erase any signs of man. Reminding himself that Bob Templeton and his boys were bent on erasing any signs of him on this earth, Rhone studied the town and mentally began to lay his defence plans while he waited for Brad Miller's stumbling, panting form to catch up with him.

★ ★ ★

They rode slowly along the middle of the street, Rhone's sharp eyes taking in every detail. There were over a dozen decaying structures, a mingling of wood and adobe, lining the street. A breeze, which rustled the horse's salt-rimmed mane, raised dust and caused sagging doors to creak on rusty hinges. When they reached an adobe church at the end of the street Rhone reined in before its low crumbling wall and nodded up at the empty belfry.

'That's a good look-out spot. We'll see them long before they git here.'

Brad slid to the ground, stared at the old church and asked dryly, 'Why do I get the feeling we are going to fight the Alamo — with the same results?'

'They didn't have repeatin' rifles at the Alamo,' Rhone said. He drew the Winchester from its saddle holster. 'But we do.' He hoisted himself from the saddle.

'And so do the outlaws,' Brad reminded him pointedly.

Rhone shrugged in dismissal and

plopped down with his back against the wall. 'We've got time for a short nap before they git here.'

'We could wake up with our throats cut!'

'Not a chance. I sleep light.'

'Who can sleep at a time like this?'

'I can,' Rhone said and closed his eyes. 'You do what you've a mind to.'

Brad stood fretting, then reluctantly sank down beside Rhone and surrendered to his weariness. He was alseep in seconds.

* * *

Phil Rhone came hard awake, suddenly goaded by the instinct of danger before the slight sound of nearby movement penetrated his consciousness. His eyes instantly flew open to see a pair of shapely bare feet attached to slim, precise ankles and long, lovely sun-bronzed legs. Slowly tilting his drooped head back against the wall, he raised his eyes.

A tall, slender young woman stood there in a man's collarless calico shirt, sleeves rolled up above her elbows, its tail ending just above her knees. A length of clothes rope serving as a belt emphasised her trim waist and held an unsheathed knife, Arapaho by its handle. A flowing mane of golden blonde hair framed her exquisite features and fell well below her straight shoulders. High, proud cheekbones complemented her large, wide-set blue eyes and sculptured nose and chin. Her softly moulded lips were drawn in a tight line of scorn.

Rhone judged her to be about twenty or so. He also judged that she was definitely hostile, for the dark, wicked muzzle of her old Spencer rifle was pointed directly at him. Looking like a white Apache, she made a striking figure against the westering sun. Careful to keep his movements slow and unmenacing, Rhone poked an elbow into Brad's ribs.

'Hey, Brad, wake up and tell me if

I'm seein' a mirage.'

Brad groaned himself awake, saw the woman and gave a start, hitting the back of his head against the wall. He yelped, started to raise a hand to his head, then saw thc blonde's Spencer shift toward him and thought better of it.

'You're not one of them . . . ' the blonde muttered sullenly. Then she eyed both men and demanded, 'Who are you — and what are you doing here?'

'Well now, that's a mutual question,' Rhone drawled. The young woman scowled dangerously, her finger impatient on the rifle's trigger. 'All right, I'll play first,' Rhone said dryly, in an effort to conceal the uneasy knot in his stomach. An armed and angry woman can kill a body just as dead as any man. 'I'm Phil Rhone from Nacogdoches way.' She frowned, confused, and he added, 'That's east Texas.' The confusion left her face, but the scowl remained. 'And my friend here is Bradley K. Miller, Jr.

from Boston. That's in Massa — '

'I know where it is,' the blonde beauty snapped indignantly.

Rhone shrugged and continued. 'Anyhow, he's rich . . . so I'd think twice about shootin' him if I was you.' Her frosty expression clearly said that she was unimpressed. 'At the moment we're runnin' for our lives from some pretty mean outlaws.'

'Don't you mean the law?'

'It's the truth!' Brad put in desperately.

'Suppose we wait and see,' the blonde said coolly.

'Then we'll all end up dead,' Rhone said flatly. She did not appear concerned. 'Us they'll just kill,' he said and gave a casual shrug. 'But you . . . ' he paused and ran his eyes up and down her tall, magnificent figure, 'now that's a different story.' He grinned wickedly. 'A long and very unpleasant one.'

The blonde only sighed and wrinkled her lovely nose disdainfully. 'You're becoming tiresome.'

'Have it your way. I just hope they

let us live long enough to watch — so I can say 'I told you so'.' She went rigid and Rhone could almost see sparks flying from her big blue eyes. That was good. If he could get her mad enough, without getting himself shot in the process, she would become careless. One tiny mistake was all he needed. To his surprise Brad was the one who caused it.

'Look, we are all civilised people . . .' Brad began, sitting forward, his hands gesturing emphatically. The rifle muzzle swivelled toward him — and that moment of distraction was all Rhone needed.

Grabbing a handful of dirt and dust, Rhone tossed it up into the blonde's face. She gave a startled cry and reeled back, blinded. He lunged up after her. She heard his movement and swung the rifle toward him. He deflected it with a swipe of his hand and felt the slug whisk past his ear, too close for comfort. He grabbed the rifle before she could jack another shell into its chamber and cock the hammer, but instead of struggling for possession she released it and stepped forward, ramming a knee up into his groin.

Rhone immediately felt a sickening agony race up through his middle. He gasped and his knees buckled under him, but he did not go down. Fighting back the pain that threatened to tear his insides apart, he put his remaining strength behind an uppercut and caught the struggling blonde squarely under her jaw. The force lifted her up on her bare toes and hurled her backward like a drunken ballerina, to fall gracelessly in a tumbled, unconscious heap on the dusty ground. Rhone continued to stave off the anguish for another few seconds to be sure she was not shamming.

She wasn't.

Rhone let his breath out in a painful sigh and finally allowed his watery legs to carry him down. He crashed heavily to his knees, hunched over and, clutching at the hurt, muttered a string of incoherent oaths directed mainly at the unconscious woman.

Brad rushed to Rhone and leaned over him. 'Are you all right?'

Rhone raised his head and eyed him disgustedly. 'Hell no, of course not!' Brad fidgeted sheepishly. Rhone feebly waved toward his horse. 'Take the saddle rope and start tying that hellcat before she wakes up. I'll help you as soon as I'm able.'

'I've never tied up a woman before,' Brad said, plainly embarrassed at the thought.

'We ain't playin' kid games. She has to be out of the way before Templeton and his hardcases git here — you *do* remember them, don't you?' The threat of danger hit home. Without another word Brad turned and hurried to the horse. Rhone returned to his misery and wondered just what he was going to do with both Bradley K. Miller, Jr. and the antagonistic blonde when the outlaws did arrive.

Well, there was no sense getting headaches ahead of time.

3

Susan Prescott woke with an aching jaw and a queasy stomach. Slowly she realised that she was lying uncomfortably on her side, her cheek pressed against the dusty earth. She remained motionless until full consciousness gradually returned, then carefully parted her long sable lashes and peeked out through their spidery effect. Her dishevelled hair partly masked one eye and she groggily squinted through its golden maze.

She saw the man who had knocked her unconscious sitting a few yards away against the adobe wall. Saddlebags between his spraddled legs, he was wolfing down a tin of meat and using a fork. Somehow, she expected he would be using his fingers. His Winchester lay on one side of him, her knife and rifle on the other.

Susan subtly stirred and instantly

felt a simultaneous tug at her crossed wrists and ankles. Her slender fingers cautiously fluttered about and confirmed what she had already guessed: she was helplessly tied hand and foot. She tensed, fear gripping her with a vengeance, then involuntarily flinched as a strong gust of wind whipped dust into her face.

The man looked up from his tin and grinned. 'Well now, I'm powerful glad to see you're back amongst us,' he said between mouthfuls and glanced up at the darkening sky. 'Looks like we're fixin' to have a big blow.'

Blinking the dust from her eyes, Susan raised her head and scowled as she writhed against her ropes. 'Damn you, untie me!'

Chewing, Rhone shook his head, then swallowed and said, 'We hafta talk first.'

'We have *nothing* to talk about,' Susan cried. She tried to squirm to a sitting position, only to find that she was further hindered by ropes above her knees and around her arms. 'When I get free . . . ' she began furiously, fingers tugging at the taut rope joining her wrists and ankles.

'You'll do nothin',' Rhone interrupted, 'but settle down and listen.' Despite her rage Susan could not stop her stomach from growling as she longingly watched him take the last bite of meat and set the tin and fork aside. 'Now, outside of a sore jaw — which you asked for — ' Rhone said pointedly, 'we haven't hurt you any.'

'These ropes are hurting me,' Susan said sullenly, her lithe muscles trembling as she strained at the imprisoning loops.

'You're doin' that yourself.' Susan glared at him indignantly and started to reply, then checked her temper. Rhone rummaged inside a saddlebag pocket. 'A mess of bandits is gonna come bustin' in here any time, and there'll be one helluva fight.' Susan eyed him narrowly as he withdrew a bandanna. 'You sure don't deserve it, but I'm givin' you a choice.'

'Oh?' Susan said, her lovely face mirroring suspicion.

Rhone nodded. 'We can't afford to fight two enemies at once, so you either fight with us or stay tied like you are.'

'Why should I help you?' Susan asked sourly.

' 'Cause you'd be helpin' yourself. You know damn well what will happen to you if they win.' She met his eyes with arctic indifference. He made another try. 'You ain't been killed or ill-used — that oughta prove we're the 'good' folk.' Her expression did not change.

'Rhone, I see them,' Brad called from above. Susan craned her slender neck and stared up at the church belfry framed against the gloomy sky as Brad leaned out, pointing excitedly.

'How far?' Rhone asked.

'About a mile. It's hard to tell with the dust.'

'All right. Come on down and let's

get ready.' Rhone stood and, twirling the bandanna into a long, thin strip, walked to Susan who lay watching him in uncertainty. 'Well, what is it to be?' he demanded, dropping to one knee. She stared up at him icily. 'Suit yourself,' he drawled and thrust the cloth between her pouting lips. Susan uttered muffled protests and wildly shook her head, trying to dislodge the gag with her tongue, as he tied it tightly at the back of her head, catching a few strands of yellow hair in the knot. Then he stood and walked back to his rifle and saddlebags at a deliberately slow pace.

Susan made a frenzied assault on her ropes, then realised the futility and, reluctantly surrendering to common sense, emitted an urgent, muffled cry. Rhone picked up his Winchester and turned to her. Large blue eyes wide and imploring above her gag, Susan frantically nodded her head in agreement.

'Now you're finally gittin' some

horse-sense,' Rhone said dryly. Susan glared venom but continued nodding. He set the rifle against the wall, picked up her knife from beside his saddlebags and ambled back to her. She squirmed impatiently and muttered unintelligibly. From her intensity Rhone was sure her words were far from flattering. 'Let's just save the bandanna for last,' he drawled. 'Maybe by then you'll have decided to act like a high-bred little lady.' Susan gave a frustrated shriek and raised her eyes to the heavens. Rhone grinned and leaned over her with the knife.

Lowering her smouldering eyes, Susan lay tense as Rhone severed the short rope connecting her bound wrists and ankles. She sighed her relief and slowly straightened her cramped legs. Then she allowed him to turn her onto her stomach and forced herself to remain very still while he deftly went to work on the other ropes.

* * *

The twelve men came with the ho
wind. Shoulders hunched agains
hammering sand and surface grit
halted at the edge of town for a
war council. Then they split into
groups and, weapons ready, caut
rode into town in search of their
Crouched in their respective po
around the street, Rhone, Bra
Susan squinted through the bli
smothering dust at the app
horsemen. Hats pulled low, b
masking the lower halves of
the riders continually va
reappeared through th
clouds.

Brad Miller presse
of a rotting building
a general store. Th
his hand and did
He had never fi
much less with
that he was fac
mind reeled at
Fear threatene
Brad forced

and fought against the nausea
izziness that weakened his knees.
diately his mouth tasted gritty
e wanted to sneeze. He wondered
one and the blonde felt this
fear. No, Rhone certainly was
raid to kill. He did not think
oman was either, not from the
e had tried to put a bullet into
He was the only coward here,
would have to overcome his
a was depending on him.

* * *

itted eyes through the
church wall, Rhone
ws' slow approach.
dly up the middle
other two groups
sides, checking
as they went.
vo side groups
Brad and the
raised up and
le group as fast

as he could jack the shells into
Winchester. The exploding shots v
muffled by the roaring wind and
the bright gunflashes and the r
recoil against his shoulder told Rl
that he was firing. The frantic a
mutely playing out in front of
further confirmed it.

One man spilled from his s
and fell beneath another rider's r
horse, whose stamping hoofs
out any life that might have
in him. Firing wildly, the
men whirled and gallope
the swirling dust clouds.
was lifted clear of his
a boot wedged in th
dragged along the
his terrified horse.
excitedly gave cov
sides of the stree

Rhone ducke
crawling to a
furious salvo
only hoped tha
blonde would j

nkly, he did not put much faith in
er of them.

★ ★ ★

h constricted in his chest, Brad
listening to the muffled gunfire
the driving wind. It had started
ie was still shaking like a leaf.
did not get a grip on himself
ld very easily become the next
n.
suddenly raced past and
fore Brad could raise the
nother man turned the
building and his horse
at the sight of him.
passed while the two
ozen, each waiting
move. Brad saw
tch as his rifle
at him. The
y and bucked
before he was
had pulled the

His own shot burrowing into the dirt before Brad's foot, the outlaw catapulted backward from his rearing horse and sprawled spead-eagled in the dirt, a large bloody hole in the middle of his chest. The frightened horse bolted down the alley as the man's body spasmed, then was still.

Eyes wild in horrid disbelief, Brad stared down at the corpse he had made. His chest rose and fell with ragged breathing as his stomach turned over and tried to rise up. He squelched it with sheer determination. There would be plenty of time for sickness and remorse after this was over; right now he had to concentrate on surviving. Brad wrenched his eyes from the dead man and forced his attention back to the raging battle as a piercing scream reached him from directly across the street.

There was a momentary break in the swirling sand and Brad saw a bandit reel out from the side of a building and collapse, the left side of his shirt stained with crimson. The blonde's shirttailed figure quickly disappeared around the back of the building, presumably to take up another position. It dawned on Brad that he should do the same.

A gaunt, bearded face unexpectedly appeared around the corner of the building with a jingling of spurs. Guided once again by his survival instinct, Brad fired without thinking. The face instantly dissolved into bloody ruin. Brad whirled and made for the rear of the building. No shots screamed after him, so evidently the others were not that anxious to avenge the two dead men.

Rounding the corner, he flattened himself against the building and, ignoring the stinging sand, stood trying to compose his raw nerves. The gunfire and dying screams out in the street did not help. A slug suddenly sent wood flying from the corner of the building. Brad whispered a curse as a long splinter drove into his shoulder. Wincing, he plucked it out and stared at the bloody tip. He hoped to hell this would be the only wound he received in the fight.

Voices and running footsteps rushed past on the boardwalk in front of the building, heading toward the church. Some of his fear drained away as Brad realised no one was stalking him. Discarding the splinter, he ran along the back of the building and carefully edged around the corner, planning to come out behind the men. As he neared the street the firing stopped. For a long moment he heard only the sighing wind. Unsettling questions ran riot through his mind.

What if he was the only one left to continue the fight!

Victorious howls jerked Brad from his panicked thoughts. He saw three men break cover and rush toward the church. No shots greeted them.

Damn it, Rhone must be dead!

★ ★ ★

Rhone let the three men charge into the courtyard then stepped into the church doorway and cut loose with his Winchester, levering it rapidly. The men ran straight into a wall of flying lead and, bodies jerking grotesquely, misdirected weapons wildly kicking up showers of dirt, sprawled in awkward postures of sudden, violent death. Rhone pumped several more rounds into them before stepping outside; a dying man can kill you just as dead as a healthy one.

Instinct made him suddenly whirl, rifle at his hip, and he found himself face to face with Bob Templeton. Simultaneously two hammers clicked sharply on empty chambers. For an instant both men gaped in stunned disbelief. With a vicious oath the big man hurled his empty six-gun at Rhone and rushed forward. Metal rang against metal as Rhone batted the pistol aside with his raised barrel and then brought the butt down a second too late. Templeton's head smashed into

Rhone's belly, driving him into the doorframe, and the rifle fell from his hands. Rhone pivoted away, swinging a fist that crashed into the side of the outlaw's head and knocked him off balance.

The big man recovered and charged, both arms flailing, forcing Rhone back inside the church. Rhone managed to duck a wild left but caught a glancing right on the jaw that set him back on his heels. Bobbing and weaving, he continued to give ground under the weight of Templeton's utter savagery as the brawny man bored in, hurling each punch with all the strength of his thick shoulders. Above the bandanna partly masking his face Templeton's dark, glittering eyes reflected a rage that went beyond hatred and seemed to be trying to destroy Rhone all by themsleves.

Rhone's fist shot out and the connecting blow sent a meaty echo through the large room. Templeton only shook his shaggy head and crowded in, giving

Rhone no time to set himself. Rhone desperately avoided a huge fist and felt the rush of air as it whisked past his head. He buried a left into the burly man's midriff and smashed a right to his heart. Still Templeton came at him with a mean stubbornness, absorbing the punishment dealt him. Rhone hooked a left to his ear, gave back, then lunged forward, putting everything he had into a savage right to the bandit's mouth. He felt his knuckles split the brute's lips apart under his bandanna, but the blow failed to dent Templeton's killing fever.

Fall, damn you! Rhone mentally yelled in frustration, aware that his punches were hurting the big man.

Templeton waded in, his fist ripping viciously across Rhone's cheekbone. Pain raked along the side of Rhone's face. Then a knee slammed up into his crotch and his body was instantly bathed in raw fire. Rhone stumbled back, weak and sick. Pressing his advantage, the big man rammed a forearm hard against Rhone's throat and followed it with a brutal haymaker.

Lightning streaked before Rhone's eyes, accompanied by a blinding red haze. His knees buckled and he went down heavily, retching for breath. Through pain-blurred eyes he saw Templeton lumber forward and then leap high in the air, to stomp him with both boot heels. Using his last shreds of strength, Rhone rolled aside an instant before the man's heavy boots struck the spot where he had lain. The sound was like a cannon's roar.

Fighting for breath, Rhone painfully struggled to his knees as Templeton, spurs jingling, menacingly stalked toward him. A fist to the forehead sent agony rippling through his brain and drove Rhone down flat on his back. He lay there semiconscious, dully aware that something very unpleasant was about to happen but not really knowing or caring until a long-shanked spur loomed above his face.

Convulsive terror burst through the

shuddering pain as Rhone realised that he would never be able to ward off the spur's sharp rowel in time. He was a dead man. Arms limp, he watched in fascinated dread as the deadly prongs started to descend.

4

Red dust leaped from the centre of Templeton's chest an instant before a rifle's deafening blast filled the room and reverberated from every wall. The outlaw's surprised eyes glazed and rolled up into his head as his tottering body started to fall forward like a toppled tree.

Rhone hurled himself aside as the dead man crashed face down on the filthy adobe floor. He slowly raised his eyes and saw the tall blonde, bandanna hanging loosely about her graceful neck, coolly pump a fresh cartridge into the Spencer's chamber. He pulled down his bandanna and, unable to find his voice, gave her a grateful grin. She smirked, and he realised that his face muscles weren't working like they should. He was probably grinning like a half-wit.

The rapid roar of a distant Colt

shifted Rhone's attention to the street and sent him bolting up and out to the courtyard wall. The blonde was there ahead of him. Together they stood watching as Brad Miller, firing from the corner of a nearby building, emptied the six-gun after two bandits, crouched low in their saddles, who were madly galloping out of town, partly obscured by roilling clouds of dust. He lowered the Colt and fumbled a few shells from a pants pocket.

'Forgit it,' Rhone shouted. 'They're out of range.'

'But they're getting away!' Brad called urgently.

'To hell with them,' Rhone replied, beckoning for him to join him.

'Aren't you going after them?' the blonde asked, whirling on Rhone in surprise.

'I've done enough hard ridin' today.'

'Suppose they come back?'

'I doubt that.' He saw her scepticism and motioned about at the dead men. 'I'd say we put the fear of God into them.' She favoured him with another of her sour expressions. 'If you're still feelin' blood-thirsty you can go blunderin' out into that dust after them — and maybe git yourself killed in the bargain.' He shrugged. 'As for me, I'm gittin' out of this storm.'

'That is the first sensible thing you've said,' the blonde said and aloofly walked away.

Rhone turned as Brad came stumbling up on the other side of the wall. Face still flushed with excitement, he asked, 'Rhone, are you sure we shouldn't go after — '

'Not you, too,' Rhone groaned disgustedly. Brad lowered his eyes sheepishly and held out the Colt. Rhone took it and returned it to his holster. 'Plenty of weapons lyin' around. Help yourself.'

'I . . . I've never touched a dead man,' Brad said, his face paling in revulsion.

Rhone gave a heavy sigh and nodded understandingly. 'All right, I'll git you one.' Brad managed a wan smile of gratitude. Rhone turned and saw the blonde moving among the three dead men, intently studying their faces. 'If you're fixin' to take scalps,' he called dryly, 'that lot is mine.' She ignored him and moved to the next body. Rhone shook his head and looked back to Brad. 'Let's wait this storm out inside the church.'

'Go ahead,' Brad said, his voice quavering, his face like chalk, 'there is something I have to do first.' With that he whirled, ducked down behind the wall and was sick.

Rhone grimaced at the unpleasant sounds and then remembered that he had done the same thing after his first Indian fight. It was best that Bradley K. Miller, Jr. had been initiated here, for there was bound to be more killing when they reached Free Town and tried to take back his wife. Killing was always ugly, but it became easier each time. Now that this threat was over Rhone could give Free Town his full

attention. He did not have a brillian
plan at the moment, but he sure bette
come up with one by the time they
reached the outlaw town.

Leaving Brad and the blonde to joi
him whenever they felt like it, Rhon
turned and strode toward the church
On his way he paused to collect
Henry repeating rifle from one of th
dead men. The blonde ignored h
nearby presence. He bet her idea
a good time was a moonlight wa
through a graveyard. Rhone con
on and went into the church.
he had sense enough to get
storm.

★ ★ ★

The three waited i
while the storm c
its accompanying
eeriness to Susan'
told of the murd
older brother in
four men, thei

blood-shot eye painted on his black
patch, who then left her to die in
the burning ranch house. Managing
to squirm outside, she had severed
her ropes with the Arapaho knife, one
of the articles the men had left in an
attempt to make it appear the work of
a marauding band. The shirt from the
clothesline and the old rifle in the barn
were all she had been able to salvage,
besides her horse.

'I have been tracking them for days,'
he said grimly. 'I lost their trail
ay, and with this storm there is
of ever finding it again.'

put a name to any of
asked.

th brow creased thought-
with the patch was
o . . . Sarto . . . '
lplessly. 'Something

tch should certainly
apprehend him,'
empathy with
wn tragedy.

'There is only one territorial marshal for this whole area,' Susan said bitterly. 'And to say he is ineffectual is being charitable.'

'My guess is you'll find those fellers in Free Town,' Rhone said, 'carousin' with their own kind.'

'You can't expect her to go into an outlaw town,' Brad said, stunned.

'I would go into hell to find them,' Susan said coldly.

'That's about what you'd be doin' by goin' to Free Town,' Rhone said flatly. He received one of her now familiar looks of cool indifference, which encouraged a plan he was beginning to formulate. He knew he should be ashamed of himself, but he now had the way of entering Free Town. 'That bein' the case, you're welcome to ride along with us. We're goin' there to fetch Brad's wife, and could be wc'll meet up with your bunch, too.' He silenced Brad with the full hardness of his glance before he could voice any gentlemanly concerns.

Luckily the blonde did not notice the exchange. Brow again knitted, she was weighing his words. Rhone knew the desire for revenge still burned fresh and unabated, so there was little doubt that she would take the bait.

There was a long moment of listening to the wind shriek with lessening fury as it blasted sand against the walls and through the various cracks, then Susan reached a decision. Tossing her hair back with a gesture of annoyance, she said dourly, 'I really seem to have no other choice.'

Already intimidated by Rhone's warning glance, Brad refrained from pointing out the obvious alternative. He knew it would be a waste of words anyway; Susan Prescott would no more give up her quest for vengeance than he would forsake his own vendetta. They would both ride into the jaws of death to accomplish their goals. He was puzzled as to Rhone's reason for including the girl. Rhone was certainly self-sufficient, and he had not even displayed his mercenary tendencies by offering to help her for a price. Now was not the time to question his taciturn companion, but he was determined to do so whenever they were alone.

* * *

Two hours later they started for Free Town, with Brad riding a dead outlaw's horse, Henry repeating carbine stuffed in its saddle scabbard, and wearing a fancy two-gun rig that still failed to make him feel like a cowboy. Rhone had cautioned him against drawing both Colts at once, saying, regardless of the Dime Novelists' claims, it slowed one's draw by split-seconds, which often made the difference in a gunfight. No Wild Bill Hickok, Brad knew he would have trouble pulling one six-gun without shooting himself in the foot, much less trying to draw both at once.

His ego further suffered from not being a proficient horseman. Having lost part of the day, Rhone set a relentless pace that had him lagging behind and receiving occasional dark scowls from an impatient Susan Prescott, who easily kept abreast of the tall cowboy. He tried reminding himself that the girl had been raised on a ranch, but it was still galling to be the 'tenderfoot' of the group.

Seeking to momentarily relieve his aching posterior, Brad dared standing in the stirrups of his fast-jogging horse, a death-grip on the saddle horn, and stared past the out-distancing riders at the slowly changing terrain. The sky was dark in the distance as the storm swept far ahead of them, and the dust-tainted air masked the sun with a rosy hue. Clumps of bushes and an occasional stunted cottonwood tree dotted the landscape as they entered the high desert country. It was a relief from the previous starkness, and the climb was gradual, almost unnoticed until he looked back in the direction from which they had come. The change in temperature was also unnoticed. Perhaps it was a few degrees cooler, but the arid heat still persisted without relief.

Brad winced as he plopped back down on the uncomfortable leather saddle harder than he had intended. The sharp slap was loud in the silence and he was embarrassed to see that Susan Prescott had been watching. Her amused smile had a hard edge to it. Drumming his heels into his horse's sides, Brad strove to close the widening distance separating him from his companions. He finally did when they dismounted and began to lead their blowing horses.

Neither Rhone nor Susan broke their long silence as Brad lowered himself heavily to the ground and flexed his shaky legs. His bones felt bruised by the endless jogging, and he could swear they were pulling free from their anchoring muscles. But worst of all was his rump, which he refrained from massaging because of Susan's presence.

He fell in on the other side of Rhone and tried unsuccessfully to match his easy, longlegged stride; he did almost manage to keep up with Susan Prescott. Again reminding himself that the two were used to hard, outdoor living, Brad struggled on and took petty delight in imagining Rhone and Susan in polite Boston society, where they would be as out of place as he was out here. It was entertaining for a time, until he remembered that he had chosen to make a new life in the West and he was the one who should learn to adjust.

San Francisco was reputed to be a city of culture and society, but it had its seedier areas such as the notorious Barbary Coast. He and Lorna could not isolate themselves in the shelter of only one part of the sprawling city for ever. While he had no intention of becoming a gunfighter, he knew he must become a much harder man than he was now to cope with the denizens of the city. He had made a start back at the ghost town, though the memory was still too fresh for him to derive satisfaction. Still, when he and Lorna were safely reunited, the experience with Rhone could then be regarded as a valuable and necessary learning lesson.

Brad groaned inwardly as Rhone soon gave an order to mount. He dragged himself up and gingerly settled himself in the saddle, ready to endure new torments. Rhone and Susan set off at a fast trot that increased to a canter and he was once more left behind to breathe their dust. Disregarding his protesting posterior, Brad slammed his heels into his horse's ribs and sent it bolting after them. This time he almost managed to keep up.

The sun was low in the rose and yellow sky when Rhone at last called a halt and announced they would 'camp a spell'. Lagging spirits renewed, Brad dragged himself from the saddle and cheerfully gathered firewood while Rhone saw to the horses and Susan set about rummaging through the supplies in all three saddlebags; it was tacit that they now belonged to all. Brad made a fire (he was at least capable of doing that) and then watched as Susan silently prepared the meal with a brisk efficiency that reminded him of Lorna. Rhone said they would have to forego coffee, as they would not reach a stream until noon tomorrow, so the scant meal of beans, hardtack, jerky and a shared tin of corned beef was sparingly washed down by water from their canteens.

The sun was sinking behind the distant mountains, moulding their hard contours into deceptive softness and staining the sky with a spectrum of flaming colours, as the three lounged about the fire, messware scattered about them. Then the moment of contentment was broken as Rhone shoved himself to his feet and announced he would saddle the horses.

'I thought we were camping for the night?' Brad asked, bewildered, dreading to climb back atop that instrument of torture called a saddle so soon. He glanced to Susan as a possible ally, but she was already scowering her tin plate clean with sand in preparation to leave.

'This ain't the safest country,' Rhone said patiently. 'Smart traveller cooks his meal, then moves on, in case somebody's seen his smoke, and makes night camp somewhere's else.'

Brad had to agree with Rhone's logic. He began helping Susan with the tinware while Rhone saddled the horses. Then he watched as Susan, evidently as cautious as Rhone, buried the glowing coals with sand and brushed over the surface with a stray branch.

Rhone led off and they rode on through the faint starlight, maintaining a steady gait but frequently shifting their trail. After several miles they came upon a nest of rocks and thick surrounding bushes and finally made their night camp. Brad was grateful to spread his blanket and escape into the oblivion of sleep. On the other side of the clearing Susan Prescott, cocked rifle beside her, did the same. Only Rhone lay awake, listening to a night bird's cry and the distant, mournful yelping of a coyote, while staring across at Susan Prescott's yellow hair billowing above her blanket and reflecting the moonlight.

It had been a long, lonely time since he had seen a woman's face in the firelight, watched her prepare a meal, much less been in her company. Tonight Susan Prescott had caused a longsuppressed, bittersweet memory to begin once more stirring in his mind. And again he willfully blocked it out. Though it had been three years it was still too soon; the scar was as fresh as the young blonde's recent tragedy. He must let the past rest and stay clear of mind if any of them were going to survive what lay ahead tomorrow.

Rhone felt a pang of guilt at his plan, but there was no other way to ride into that outlaw town without a challenge. If things went right Bradley K. Miller,

Jr. would be reunited with his stolen bride, and Susan Prescott might even take her revenge on the one-eyed man. If things went the other way he and Brad would be dead, and Susan would join Lorna Miller in a life of slavery, to an outlaw or a bordello owner.

Telling himself that staying awake all night worrying would resolve nothing, Rhone put his head down on the pillowing saddle and went to sleep. Sometime during the night Susan Prescott crept into his dreams. He could not remember the details, only that it was very enjoyable.

5

They were up at the crack of dawn and on the trail before full sun-up. Rhone set a swift pace, trying to take advantage of the coolness of morning, and Brad did a better job of keeping up than he had done yesterday. Susan Prescott was almost cheerful for a change, but never having fully cultivated the art of conversation (especially around beautiful women), Rhone was not able to take good advantage of her rare mood. He envied Brad's easy manner and gift for words as he enthralled Susan with tales of Boston and the East, a world so alien to a small rancher's daughter.

Shortly after noon they reached a narrow stream, stretched out on the bank and drank, then filled their canteens to overflowing before allowing the horses to drink. Rhone plopped down in the shade with his back against a cottonwood tree and watched from under his low pulled hat brim while Susan bathed her face, neck and arms with a wet bandanna, then waded into the stream and began to wash the trail dust from her long, perfect legs. Before he got to enjoying the view too much Brad walked up and obscured it. Rhone irritably felt like telling him that he made a better door than a window.

'How much farther is it to Free Town?' Brad asked, running a wet cloth around inside the hatband of his derby.

Thumbing his hat off his forehead, Rhone raised his eyes to Brad's face. 'We oughta git there a bit after sundown.'

'Then we steal in and find Lorna?'

'Somethin' like that,' Rhone said with a noncommittal shrug.

Brad glanced back at Susan who was now standing in the calf-deep water and wringing the wet bandanna down under the front of her calico shirt, relishing its cool trickles on her skin. 'Won't Miss Prescott be a hindrance?'

'No.'

'But we cannot do two things at once — and we certainly cannot abandon her there.'

'We won't.' Rhone pulled the brim back down over his forehead. 'Now you just leave all the frettin' to me, and do as you're told when we go in there.' Brad hesitated, wanting to hear more, but Rhone had no further words of comfort and ended the conversation. 'Why don't you fetch some wood and we'll git us a cookfire goin'?' As Brad turned and trudged off, Rhone stared after him and secretly wished he felt as confident as he had appeared; but long ago he had learned that nothing in life was ever certain.

They ate leisurely and lingered over Susan's good coffee, letting the heat of the day pass. Free Town was not that far away and Rhone did not want to arrive there until after dark. By then its inhabitants should be well liquored up and careless, making their task a little easier.

Crossing the stream, they turned west and rode toward the looming mountain range which no longer appeared deceptively remote. Still night fell before they reached the foothills that seemed to stretch endlessly before it. Rhone hurried the pace some but kept a wary watch for men concealed in the long dark shadows or atop a hill or boulder. Soon faint random gunshots reached them. Rhone disregarded his companions' enquiring glances and pressed on. They had not gone far before the fainter roar of many voices was heard accompanying the sporadic gunfire.

'Is there an Indian attack?' Brad asked, low, straining to make out Rhone's features beneath the dark shadow cast by his wide brim.

'Just folks havin' fun,' Rhone replied and gigged his mount forward, leaving his companions to follow suit.

Cresting a rise, they looked down

on a one-street town, with mainly low, flat buildings ranged along its length on either side, about a half-mile away. Lights showed through windows along most of the torch-lit street that was fairly teeming with rowdy people. Whooping and firing six-guns in the air, a group of drunken riders raced up and down the street, scattering anyone in their path and bringing laughter from the onlookers.

'So that is Free Town,' Brad said, eyeing the activity uncomfortably.

'Yeah,' Rhone said. 'Nice, quiet little community, ain't it?'

'How do we get in there?'

'We ride right in,' Rhone said simply.

'That's not much of a plan,' Susan remarked sourly.

'There's more,' Rhone said, turning to her. 'Brad and me are gonna be a couple of bandits — and you're the woman we've come to sell.'

'Is that the reason you wanted me to accompany you?' Susan demanded, hurt and suspicious.

'Don't worry, we ain't gonna sell you,' Rhone said reassuringly.

'I know you won't,' Susan said, her lovely features rigid with disapproval. 'Because I refuse to do it!'

'You got a better plan?' Rhone drawled. She remained coldly silent, staring fixedly ahead at the noisy outlaw town. Rhone shrugged and said, 'Then it's all settled.'

Still intent on the town, Susan said firmly, 'I *won't* go.'

★ ★ ★

They boldly rode into town single-file, Rhone leading Susan's horse and Brad, derby set at a jaunty angle, bringing up the rear. Wrists securely fastened behind her, Susan sat glowering at Rhone's broad back, then her cold blue eyes ranged over the various hardcases, gawking with vulgar interest along the broken boardwalk, in search of her one-eyed man. Rhone scanned the street and his gaze settled on a two-storey, well-lit saloon, busy with men coming and going in varied stages of inebriation.

'That seems to be the most likely place,' Rhone called back to Brad. He pushed his horse forward and turned in to a hitch-rail on one side of the large saloon, pulling Susan's horse in with him. Brad turned in on the other side of her. Rhone dismounted and tied both horses' reins around the rail in loose knots, in case of a hasty getaway. He moved around and, acting his part, helped Susan down from the saddle none too gently. She rewarded him with one of her best dark scowls. He took her arm and steered her out into the street where Brad was waiting, keeping a worried eye on the racing horsemen, firing and hollering, as they approached down the street.

'What now?' Brad asked.

'Just look mean and leave the talkin' to me,' Rhone said before all talk was made impossible by the thundering riders. He noticed Susan intently eyeing the riders searchingly and gave a weary sigh. After the horsemen had charged on toward the end of the street, he said, 'Susan, you're supposed to be our captive — look scared, huh?'

'That is exactly what I am,' Susan said quietly.

'Then show it,' Rhone said and roughly led her toward the saloon with Brad trailing behind them.

They pushed through the sagging bat wing doors and stood surveying the large room, lighted mainly by two wagon wheel chandeliers, kerosene lamps guttering and staining the high ceiling. Men slouched in chairs around tables near a long, crowded bar lining one wall. The gaming tables were closed due to an auction in progress on the small entertainment stage at the far end of the room. To one side of the stage a staircase led up to the floor above and a railing ran the length of the wall. Double-barrelled shotgun across his lap, a saloon guard sat in a high chair near the stairs and kept an eagle eye on the stage where a gaunt man in a battered top hat, white collarless shirt and frayed frock coat and trousers was making a dignified, impassioned appeal, praising the virtues of a frightened, young Mexican woman, whose broad, swarthy features and blue-black hair revealed her mixed Indian heritage, to a boisterous, mainly unreceptive audience.

Repelled by the auction and the tough men in the front of the saloon who had noticed her and were making lewd comments, Susan unconsciously shied against Rhone. Under other circumstances he would have welcomed the feel of her soft, willowy body against him, but now was not the time to be taken as her protector. He forced himself to rudely thrust her forward and nodded to Brad. All eyes were on them as they walked the gauntlet between the bar and tables.

A burly drunk suddenly lunged from his chair and grabbed Susan as she started past. She gave a startled cry and struggled in his arms as he began trying to kiss and fondle her, drawing coarse laughter from the others. Rhone whirled to intervene but Brad, automatically acting the gentleman, jerked the drunk away from Susan and flattened him with a crashing right to his mouth. The laughter abruptly died, replaced by hostile, challenging stares. With crystal clarity Brad realised the gravity of his rash act and tensed, ready for a fight.

Thankfully the ruckus had caught the guard's attention and fear of his twin-barrelled shotgun quickly defused the explosive situation. The groaning drunk groggily shoved himself up on an elbow and wiped the back of his hand across his bloody mouth.

Dragging Susan with him, Rhone stepped to Brad's side and threw a hard, sweeping glance about at the silent men. 'No samplin' the goods before auction,' he said flatly. The surrounding faces remained sombre but there was no challenge. He was about to turn away with Susan when the drunk yanked a Bowie knife from his boot tip.

In a seemingly casual motion Rhone pivoted and kicked a long leg straight out. The toe of his boot caught the man under the point of his unshaven chin as he started to rise, violently snapped his head back between his shoulders and hurled him flat on the floor, the large knife slipping from his limp hand.

Again Brad tensed expectantly, but the guard's scattergun still held sway.

Turning from the senseless man, Rhone seized a huge handful of Susan's cascading hair, bringing her up on bare tiptoes with a pained gasp, and said gruffly, 'C'mon, you, and quit makin' trouble for folks.' With that he steered her toward the stage. His remark and rough treatment brought a few snickers from the men and removed any remaining tension.

As Brad turned and strode after Rhone there was a sudden rush behind him. He nervously whirled and was relieved to see a group of men jostling and fighting amongst themselves as each tried to lay claim on the unconscious man's valuables. That was evidently tolerated, for the shotgun guard paid no heed.

The auction had ended for a time and the disgruntled crowd was dispersing to the bar and gaming tables opening for business when Rhone, Susan and Brad reached the side of the stage near the staircase. A few lingered briefly to throw lustful glances at the tall, scantily-clad blonde beauty before drifting off. On stage the seedy auctioneer collected the last few gold coins from a big man who then took the long rope attached to the softly sobbing Mexican girl's tied wrists and led her down the few steps on the opposite side. Pocketing the coins in a coat pocket, the auctioneer eyed Susan with an obvious interest as he walked to the edge of the stage.

'You gents buying or selling?' the gaunt man asked, his voice and manner suggesting all the charm of a snake-oil salesman.

'We ain't decided,' Rhone drawled.

The man squatted and slowly ran his dark, shrewd eyes appraisingly over Susan. 'She oughta fetch a pretty penny, and I'm the man who can get it for you.' He paused and ran a bony hand over his salt and pepper stubbled chin. 'Or if you'd like, I'll buy her off you here and now — top dollar.' He nodded and looked the picture of sincerity. 'Be a whole lot quicker that way, and save all the fuss and bother of an auction.'

'We'll think on it,' Rhone said easily. He jerked a thumb toward Brad. 'Right now, my friend here had his mind set on a red-haired gal,' The auctioneer screwed up his long face in thought. Rhone looked over the top of Susan's head at Brad. 'Go ahead, partner, tell the man just what you want.' While Brad began to describe Lorna, Rhone casually half turned, resting an arm on the edge of the stage, and positioned himself so that he could watch the saloon activities.

When Brad had finished the auctioneer shook his head and was crestfallen. 'You should have been here earlier. I sold a redhead just like that to Pa Dagget.'

'Are you sure?' Brad asked anxiously.

'It's not every day I get a real high-class lady to sell. Most of them are like that last one you saw.'

Brad threw a desperate glance to Rhone, who said, unconcerned, 'Could be this Pa Dagget might be persuaded to sell her. Where do we find him?'

'That was late in the afternoon. By now he and his kin are probably on their way home, back up the mountain.'

'Perhaps we can overtake them?' Brad said to Rhone.

'Someone else has the same idea,' the auctioneer interjected. 'Just after dusk Sardo came in looking for a beautiful woman *and* Pa Dagget.' He chuckled deep in his throat. 'Take my advice and forget about that particular redhead.'

Rhone caught Brad's look of concern and also noticed Susan had forgotten her play-acting and was deep in thought. 'How come?' he asked.

'Pa's lot has been raiding Sardo's employer's gold shipments, and there is going to be 'blood on the moon' when they meet. I'm willing to bet Sardo will have both the girl and Pa's hide.'

Rhone saw Susan stiffen, her hands closing into tight fists behind her back, and understood her urgent sidelong glance. 'This Sardo,' he said casually, 'he wear a patch with a blood-shot eye on it?'

'One in the same. You know him?'

'I heard tell of him.'

The conversation was interrupted as a deep voice boomed from the front of the saloon, 'Bounty killer.' A sudden quiet fell over the huge room. Rhone turned and recognised the two men standing just inside the swinging doors as the remaining members of Bob

Templeton's gang. They had evidently come to Free Town to await any other survivors of the shoot-out.

Striding forward with his companion, the bushy-bearded man addressed the whole saloon again. 'Them two back there with the girl. The tall one is Phil Rhone, bounty hunter.' The rest of his words were lost in the crowd's savage roar as, moving as one, the men fell in behind the two.

In one fluid movement Rhone drew and put a bullet into the centre of the guard's forehead before he could bring his shotgun to bear from his commanding position atop the high chair. The man slammed back against the wall, the gun bucking from his lifeless hands as both barrels aborted into the ceiling and brought down one of the heavy waggon wheel chandeliers with a resounding crash. The mob gave back as the broken lanterns spread their contents over the worn wood floor and trails of fire spread in all directions.

'Take Susan up those stairs,' Rhone

shouted above the chaos.

Brad delayed to grab the auctioneer by his shirt front as he started to rise and pull a derringer from a coat pocket. The gaunt man gave a startled yell as he somersaulted to the floor like a great long-legged spider, spilling gold and silver coins, and landed heavily on his back. He lay stunned but Susan further ensured his incapacity by smashing a bare heel down on his stomach and driving the wind from his lungs in a rush. Brad caught Susan's arm and pulled her to the stairs.

Rhone covered their retreat by shooting holes in several of the lamps on the other hanging waggon wheel near the front of the saloon, sending kerosene spraying down on to the floor and some of the disorganised crowd. Even wilder panic ensued as the new puddles ignited and more than one man became a human torch. Rhone whirled and bolted up the staircase as shots and curses screamed after him. He gained the landing and, emptying his Colt down at the howling mob as he went, ran into the nearby hallway behind Brad and Susan.

A few doors curiously opened as the three pelted along the hall, but quickly slammed shut when the rooms' occupants saw Rhone's grim face and still smoking six-gun. Brad and Susan reached the outside door at the end of the hall and found it locked. Ordering them aside, Rhone charged up and shattered it off one hinge with a savage kick. Holstering his own Colt, Rhone pulled one from Brad's double rig as he started out the gaping doorway with Susan. Rhone shouted for them to get to their horses as the two hurried down the rickety stairs, then turned at the sound of footsteps and excited voices entering the hall from the fiery saloon area. He fanned the Colt, dropping two men and sending the rest scurrying back around the corner to safety, then spun and began pounding down the stairs.

Brad and Susan dashed along the

back of a building next to the saloon, turned into an alley on its far side and followed it to the edge of the street. Halting in the shadows, they stood gasping for breath and watching the pandemonium in the street as men, on foot and horseback, converged on the burning saloon. They spotted their horses at the tie rack in front of the building and exchanged relieved glances.

'Now all we have to do is reach them,' Brad said apprehensively. He started to fumble in search of the imprisoning knots but Susan shook her head and drew her tied wrists away.

'There is no time,' she whispered. 'Besides, if any one notices us it will look better with you leading me to the horses like I'm your prisoner.'

He considered, then nodded and they pressed farther into the shadows as a group of men stormed past on their way to the saloon. Susan looked to Brad and stepped from the alley. He took her arm and hurried her to the horses. The weathered saloon was going up like a tinder box, singed survivors staggering out through the flames and thick clouds of black, eye-stinging smoke, and the agitated crowd was too preoccupied to pay any heed as Brad helped Susan up on her saddle.

'What about Rhone?' he asked, taking her reins and swinging aboard his nervous horse.

'He is more than able to take care of himself,' Susan said, glancing back at the blazing saloon as showering sparks threatened the nearby buildings. 'I am sure he will catch up with us.'

The street was now devoid of racing horsemen, and Brad pushed their mounts forward at a fast trot. They were at the edge of town when he heard a rider and looked around to see Rhone galloping after them. He also saw that more buildings were on fire, engaging the crowd's complete attention. Brad slowed his pace and Rhone easily overtook them.

Drawing in beside Brad, Rhone reached over and took Susan's reins. 'Put your spurs to that bronc,' he said hurriedly, 'and let's git while the gittin' is good.' He touched his heels to his horse's flanks and galloped ahead with Susan.

Brad had no spurs but he well understood Rhone's meaning and followed his example. They tore out of town and off into the night while the tumult raged behind them.

★ ★ ★

'They'll sure remember us this night in Free Town,' Rhone remarked cheerfully as they sat their winded horses and looked back from a hilltop at the distant outlaw town in flames. 'For a long spell, too,' he added.

'If there is anything left of Free Town,' Brad said, still flush from all the excitement.

'It was a night I could have done without,' Susan said sulkily, rubbing her slim, rope-marked wrists.

'I'd say we made out right well,' Rhone said easily, trying to banter Susan out of her mood. 'You learned the name of your one-eyed man, and we found out what we needed to know.' Susan only made a wry face. Saddle leather creaking, Rhone turned and stared toward the mountain looming against the starry sky. 'What we all want is up there, so it looks like we'll still be travellin' together — unless you're of a different mind?' Susan looked at him without any change of expression, then shook her head. Her beautifully unruly blonde hair made ripples in the pale light.

'I only hope we can get Lorna away from this Pa Dagget before Susan's man, Sardo, finds him,' Brad said, becoming serious. 'I hate to think of her trapped in the middle of a gunfight.'

'Sounds like Sardo has a good head start on us,' Rhone said, 'but we'll do our best to git there first.'

'And if we don't?' Brad asked uneasily.

'Let's cross that bridge when we come to it,' Rhone replied confidently.

For a time the three silently stared at the towering mountain now easily within their reach, each lost in private speculation about the outcome of the individual dramas soon to take place somewhere up in its dark pine and white aspen forests. Then Rhone wordlessly put his horse forward at a walk and Brad and Susan sombrely fell in behind him.

6

Lorna Miller's respectable life in Boston had ill-prepared the young red-haired beauty for the various nightmarish worlds into which she had been forceably thrust, beginning only a few short days ago with her abduction from her husband by their guide and his half-breed helper. Awakened at false dawn by a rough hand clamping over her mouth Lorna had been pulled, struggling, from her blankets, placed on her horse, hands tied behind her back, bare feet fastened to the stirrups, and taken endlessly across the desert to Free Town. There she had been humiliatingly auctioned on a saloon stage to the highest bidder: a lean, grizzled man called Pa Dagget. Bound like one of the surrounding sacks of provisions she had been deposited in the back of a buckboard and taken up into the mountains by Pa Dagget and six rough men, whom she learned were relatives of one sort or another.

Now they were camped off the trail in a hollow surrounded by sage and forest and tucked away between two timbered, high-humped hills. She was uncomfortably lashed against a rear wheel of the buckboard, ropes around her torso, wrists attached behind her to a spoke, legs extended and tied together at the knees and trim ankles. Her white blouse and green riding skirt had long been reduced to tatters that were a mockery of propriety, and she was shivering in the cool night air while her captors comfortably lounged around a campfire, eating, drinking and talking in coarse language that was suited to the Boston docks.

Despite her discomfort Lorna managed to doze, only to be soon awakened by loud, nearby drunken laughter. She raised her drooped head and saw two young men staggering toward her, passing a whisky bottle back and forth;

more of its contents seemed to run down their stubbled chins than into their mouths.

'Hey, you good-lookin' thing, you,' said the taller of the two, a gangling, dark-haired man with a long-jawed, narrow face.

'She don't appear to like us none, Ferret,' said the other, a short barrel of a man whose round legs almost split his denims, as Lorna coldly turned her head aside and stared at the darkness beyond the clearing.

'She'll like us just fine, Jubal,' Ferret said as he lurched up and squatted down beside Lorna, 'after she's done had a little somethin' to drink.' Lorna shied with a gasp as he thrust the saliva-wet bottle neck in her face. She turned her head aside but found herself staring into Jubal's grinning moon face.

'Aw, c'mon and drink with us,' the squat man coaxed. 'There ain't no call to be uppity, 'cause you're gonna be our kin.'

'Sure enough,' Ferret confirmed.

Lorna looked from one snickering face to another and shook her head in revulsion. She gave a sharp cry as Jubal roughly grabbed a pudgy fistful of her long hair and forced her head back against a hard wheel spoke, then gagged as Ferret shoved the bottle neck into her open mouth, almost breaking her teeth, and pouring the raw liquor down her throat. Lorna coughed and vainly tried to shake her head as the liquid overflowed her mouth and ran down her chin and neck. That only amused her tormentors, and Ferret continued to force her to drink.

A bullwhip cracked like a pistol shot. Jubal yowled and leaped up as the braided leather whacked across his meaty rump. Startled, Ferret dropped the bottle which leaked some of its contents onto Lorna's lap before rolling to the ground.

'Ferret . . . Jubal, git yourselves on away from her,' Pa Dagget bawled, snaking the long black whip back across the ground. 'You know she's to be

Reese's woman!'

'Pa, that smarted somethin' fierce,' Jubal complained, clutching both buttocks.

'Well, I can make it smart more,' Dagget snarled and stalked forward.

'It was Ferret's idea, Pa,' Jubal whined, pointing an accusing finger at his brother, who shot him a murderous glance.

'I don't care whose idea it was,' Dagget said harshly, stopping before them.

'Aw, Pa,' Ferret said, forcing a weak smile, 'what's the harm in us gettin' to know her first?'

'I bought her for Reese — not you two.'

'He's just gonna kill her durin' one of his damn fits,' Jubal said, pointing down at Lorna as she recovered from coughing.

'Yeah, just like he done them other three women you bought for him,' Ferret put in.

'He's a squirrel,' Jubal said.

Lorna raised her head and stared up at the men with wide, frightened eyes as her confused mind grasped the importance of their conversation. She was overwhelmed by fear and despair much worse than anything else she had endured since her abduction at the thought of being a gift for a murderous lunatic.

'Don't be talkin' that way about your older brother,' Dagget cautioned. 'He's gonna be head of this family when I'm gone.'

'You always liked him better,' Ferret said defensively, 'but face it, Pa, he's — '

'Hush up,' Dagget growled. 'Now the both of you git!'

'But our bottle?' Jubal protested, pointing down at the overturned bottle spilling its contents in a widening puddle beside Lorna.

'You've had too much already,' Dagget said disgustedly and drew back the whip for emphasis. He stood glaring as the two begrudgingly shuffled away, muttering incoherently, then sent the whip cracking after them. With startled oaths both men broke into mad runs. Dagget grinned, picked up the bottle and hurled it off toward the bushes. 'They're drunk,' he said to Lorna. 'Don't pay them no never-mind.' Coiling the whip around one shoulder, he hunkered down beside Lorna. 'You and Reese will git on fine.' He reached out and stroked her cheek with the back of a hand. She went rigid at his touch. He grinned and went on pleasantly, trying to soothe her apprehension. 'You'll give him lots of big, strong sons to run things after him.'

Lorna recoiled from his touch and shook her head defiantly. 'No. I . . . I shan't!'

Dagget's pleasant manner abruptly vanished. His pale eyes became baleful and wicked. 'You'll do what I tell you, missy.'

Lorna glared back at him with utter loathing, hating the patriarch and his family with every fibre of her being.

Somehow that hatred gave her strength. 'I will not bear the child of a filthy madman!'

The back of Dagget's hand suddenly whipped out with blurring speed and cracked loudly across Lorna's face. She gave a cry of shocked pain as her head violently rocked to one side. He angrily lunged to his feet. 'By damn, girl, you're gonna learn here and now,' he said, uncoiling the bullwhip, 'not to sass me or speak disrespectful of my kin.'

Lorna tilted her head and stared up at him with stunned green eyes. A thin trickle of blood wormed out of one corner of her bruised mouth. She cringed hard against the wheel spokes as he threw his arm back unravelling the long whip, and bit her lower lip, determined not to give him the satisfaction of begging for mercy. The wild glow on his weathered face plainly told that this was a pleasure he would not be denied. She tensed expectantly, resigned to the pain that was to come.

A shotgun roared from the nearby bushes. A crazy red pattern appeared in Dagget's chest as he was abruptly lifted right out of one boot and catapulted to the ground flat on his back. Lorna stared in wide-eyed confusion at the empty boot standing before her. Then her attention was wrenched away as the clearing exploded into violence.

Led by a tall man in black, wearing a patch with a horrid blood-shot eye painted on it, a group of men burst from the surrounding darkness, yelling and firing rifles and six-guns. Though outnumbered the six remaining Dagget clan put up a hard fight, whittling down the odds. Stinging eyes and assailing nostrils with its acrid smell, gunsmoke blanketed the clearing like fog and was punctured by the red and yellow flashes of various loudly discharging weapons.

Unable to escape the sights and sounds about her, Lorna jerked her legs up to her body and cowered against the waggon wheel. Everywhere she looked men's partially obscured shapes moved like grotesque spectres, cursing, screaming, dying, weapons still blazing in their death throes and adding even more pungent smoke to the air.

Abruptly it was over, the last echoing shots racketting off into the night, and the momentary quiet was startlingly loud. Then the vacuum was filled by the groans of the wounded or dying. The shooting began anew as the attackers moved through the dissipating clouds of gunsmoke, ending the misery of friend and foe alike.

Huddled tremblingly against the waggon wheel, Lorna saw Ferret, bleeding profusely, lying propped up on an elbow clicking an empty pistol at the slowly approaching tall, one-eyed man in black who, smoking Colt dangling at his side, ignored him and stared directly at her. As he passed, the one-eyed man, in almost a careless gesture, turned his Colt down and shot Ferret in the face without a break in stride. Lorna uttered a sharp cry at the casual act of violence and, slender wrists twisting and straining at the encircling ropes, vainly attempted to press through the spokes and take shelter underneath the waggon.

Then the man was standing before her. Her distorting curtain of red hair seemed to make his image even more frightening. His dark eye slowly crawled over her from head to bare toes while his awful painted eye seemed to stare straight through her. Breath trapped in her chest, Lorna could only remain rigid and stare up at him in wide-eyed, perverse fascination.

A slow smile spread over Sardo's hard features and he remarked aloud, more to himself than the cringing young redhead, 'That auctioneer was right . . .' He saw her bewilderment, then enjoyed her nervous start as he rammed the Colt back into its holster with a sharp slap of leather. 'You got nothing to fear.' He kicked over Pa Dagget's still standing boot. ' 'Twas me who saved you from a rawhiding

111

by that old bastard.' Lorna made no response. Sardo turned at the sound of nearby movement and saw a big man looting Ferret's pockets. 'Rafe, come get her up from here and tie her on a horse.'

The big man begrudgingly paused in his work and scowled over at the two. 'Aw, Sardo, why me?'

' 'Cause you're the closest,' Sardo answered simply and rested a hand on his gun butt.

The none too subtle action was not wasted on Rafe. With a heavy sigh of disgust he heaved himself up and stalked forward, blood smeared hand dribbling coins as he stuffed the plunder into a shirt pocket. Under Sardo's watchful eye he whipped a knife from its sheath on one hip and dropped down beside Lorna, who continued to shrink against the spokes.

'Handle her gentle-like,' Sardo cautioned as Rafe started on Lorna's ropes. 'She's to be Mister Forbes' new woman.'

'Do tell?' Rafe commented, his surly manner vanishing. He paused to study Lorna critically, then grunted and nodded his approval. 'She sure beats Rosa six ways to Sunday.' He chuckled. 'Wonder how Rosa is gonna take being replaced?' Sardo gave a disinterested shrug. 'Not too kindly, I'll bet,' Rafe continued. 'And with that hot chili pepper temper of hers — '

'That's Mister Forbes' concern,' Sardo interrupted, his cold tone warning that the discussion was at an end. Rafe wisely fell silent and resumed wielding the knife with the utmost care as he freed Lorna from the waggon wheel. Sardo turned and bawled to the others, 'Awright, grab what you can and be quick about it. We done what needed doing, and it's a long ride back home.' He strode off, leaving Rafe to tend to Lorna.

Oblivious to Rafe's knife, Lorna sat lost in troubled thought. Questions ran rampant through her mind, but she could not bring herself to ask the uncouth man beside her. She was aware of an unsettling knot in the pit of her stomach as she grimly wondered if she had been rescued from one trial only to face an even greater and deadlier one?

* * *

From halfway up the timbered side of one of the two high-humped hills overlooking the clearing, Ed Kobeck had impartially watched the massacre. Two years' of hard labour in Nelson Forbes' mines had inured him to the plight of others. His only concern was in obtaining food. His stomach was eating its way through his backbone. He had planned to slip down and steal what he could while the first group and their woman captive were sleeping. Now his plans had been drastically changed by the arrival of the second group, and he could only hope they did not tote off everything.

Kobeck was too far away to make out

their features, but there was something familiar about the apparent leader of the second group. His leathery, weathered face slowly hardened in recognition as he watched the man in black's ramrod, military carriage while strutting about the hollow, snapping orders and hurrying his looting men.

'Sardo . . . ' he said aloud with toneless virulence. Instantly he crouched lower, fearful that his voice would carry. To his knowledge Kobeck was the last of over a dozen workers who had made a desperate escape from the mines. He had come too far and suffered too much to be caught now.

Rage and fear warring inside him, Ed Kobeck remained crouched low and continued to watch the slowly departing men in the clearing below.

7

They were up into the mountains and climbing swiftly, racing the dawn that was greying the velvet sky. Earlier there had been occasional begrudging halts to dismount and lead their wheezing horses, but now Rhone kept to a gruelling pace. With the sunrise their quarries would soon break camp, and the distance gained during night travel would again be lengthened.

Almost before they were aware of it the orange sun rose into the eastern sky, its probing rays picking out in bold relief the sharp edges of the serrated horizon. But the freshness of morning brought no relief, only greater concern, as the three rode on in single file up the twisting trail that was barely wide enough for the rutted waggon tracks they were following. Below and on either side green pine forests clung to the steep slopes, while a grey-brown rocky barrenness rose above the timberline.

For several hours of steady travel, each silent with his own thoughts, they saw no sign of human life. The wooded slopes and canyons seemed empty except for birds and an occasional deer. Then they were out of a canyon and could clearly see the sky ahead. It was filled with hovering flocks of large, dark birds.

Deep lines of tension carved Rhone's taut face as his narrowed eyes, shrouded by the wide brim of his flat-crowned hat, watched various birds swoop down to disappear behind a high-humped hill a short distance ahead. He threw a glance back at his companions. Their eyes met for a moment, reading one another's thoughts, all sensing the presence of unseen danger in the surrounding mountain forests. Wordlessly Rhone reached down, slid his Winchester from its scabbard and jacked a shell into its chamber, the noise cracking loudly in the silence. Behind him he heard Susan lever a bullet into her Spencer. Holding the rifle ready in one hand, Rhone lifted his reins and nudged his horse forward with his knees. The others followed Rhone, who kept his tall horse to a slow walk that raised little dust, away from the canyon and toward the timbered hill.

Soon they cautiously reached the crest of the hill and, staying in the shadowy trees, looked down at death scattered about in the hollow below. Attracted from miles around, ugly black buzzards were beginning to pick over the spoils. The grisly sight was not new to Rhone, but only another of nature's unpleasant reminders of man's mortality. He looked over and saw Brad go ashen; even Susan's usually dour expression slipped as a small, uncontrolled shiver shook her slender frame.

'Appears Sardo got here first,' Rhone said softly. 'But he paid a price.'

'Lorna . . . ' Brad said urgently and

started to put his horse forward.

Rhone reached out and caught his reins. 'Don't go jumpin' the gun. There's a good chance Sardo took her.'

'But . . . ' Brad began.

'That auctioneer said he was lookin' for *both* her and Pa Dagget, remember?'

'Rhone is right,' Susan said comfortingly.

Rhone was pleased to have her agreeing with him for a change. It was also nice to find that she was capable of considering other folks' feelings, after all. Brad seemed somewhat appeased so Rhone released the reins and gave his attention back to the massacre site.

As Rhone's keen eyes ranged over the hollow and its surrounding woods and bushes, he was aware of a variety of smells. Mixed with the scent of pine and that of wood slowly rotting in the damp earth was a faint trace of the odour which had brought the birds. Since buzzards liked their food ripe, they had not yet gotten down to the serious business of feasting, contenting themselves with staking claims and plucking out an eye or two. That meant Sardo probably did not have too great a lead; he would know more when he got down there and studied the tracks.

Satisfied with his scrutiny, Rhone's gaze returned to his companions. 'Wait here while I take a closer look.' The two looked a little queasy but shook their heads. 'There's nothin' but ugliness down there.'

'I have seen ugliness before,' Susan said, meeting his eyes impassively.

'So have I,' Brad said flatly.

Rhone studied their determined faces then shrugged, not wishing to waste valuable time in futile argument. 'Suit yourselves,' he said and started down the sloping hill, weaving around an occasional tree.

The stench reached Rhone halfway down the slope. His horse snorted, shook its head urgently and tried to veer off. He prodded it back on course with his knees and continued down toward the quarrelling buzzards. He heard the others struggling with their balking horses but did not look back. In the dewy, sun-screened dimness of the shaggy-trunked pines the smell of dead flesh became stronger and his mount again shied. Brad and Susan came up on either side and, holding in their snorting, skittish horses, peered past the staggered trees at the carnage ahead. Winchester cradled in his arms, finger near the trigger, Rhone forced his horse on and the others pressed close behind him.

A score of wranglesome buzzards begrudgingly took to wing with a loud flapping and shrieking as the three riders broke into the hollow. Screeching angry protests, they hovered near overhead like a black cloud, then abruptly separated and climbed higher as a startling pistol shot brought one spiralling to the ground. It flopped about for a moment, then was still, as ungainly in death as the human corpses around it.

Rhone twisted in the saddle and glared back at Brad, smoking Colt in hand, striving to control his frightened horse. 'Why the hell did you see fit to do that?' he demanded.

'I was trying to drive them away,' Brad answered, surprised by the disapproving glances from both Rhone and Susan.

'They won't come down while we're here.'

'That shot was heard for miles,' Susan explained with strained patience. Disregarding Brad's sheepish expression, she leaned forward and whispered soothingly into her nervous horse's ear.

Shaking his head and scowling his disgust, Rhone booted his unwilling mount forward and trotted across the hollow to the buckboard. He reined in and, bracing himself for what he might see, peered down into the waggon bed. Thankfully Lorna Miller was not inside. He drew a relieved breath at the sight of provisions strewn about in wild profusion. A large flour sack lay ripped wide, its scattered contents revealed only one set of boot prints had tromped about inside. He heard a horse approaching, then Brad's voice called:

'Is Lorna . . . ' he broke off, unable to bring himself to finish the sentence, as if to do so would confirm her fate.

Rhone glanced over as Brad pulled up near him. 'I told you she's with Sardo,' he said, total conviction now in his tone. The apprehension left Brad's face, only to be replaced by concern brought by the new prospect of danger. Rhone looked past him and saw Susan, dismounted, dispassionately moving among the dead, studying each face. The scene made his scalp crawl. A corpse was not pleasant to view under normal circumstances, but with the buzzards' mutilations it was absolutely stomach-wrenching. He had to credit her grit.

'Shouldn't we find their trail and get started?' Brad impatiently suggested.

Rhone turned back and pointed down at a rear waggon wheel with severed ropes dangling from its spokes. 'That's where they kept her.' He nodded down at the other loose ropes on the ground and a woman's small bare footprints along with several sets of men's boots. 'This other bunch freed her and took her off.' He nudged his mount forward and, scanning the ground, slowly headed around the end of the buckboard.

As Brad turned his horse after Rhone he noticed a lone boot and could not keep his eyes from curiously wandering over to its owner. Immediately he wished he had not done so. The lean, grizzled man lay on his back, one arm outflung, hand clutching a bullwhip. A huge cluster of droning flies had gathered on his bloody head and chest. His eyes had been gouged out and part of his face devastated by the sharp-beaked carrion birds.

Tasting bile in his throat, Brad quickly averted his eyes and saw

Susan, oblivious to the thick, buzzing swarms of flies that rose in annoyance from every corpse she inspected, still continuing her grim search. He marvelled at her constitution. The sight of one disfigured corpse was more than enough for him. He turned away and rode to join Rhone.

Though sickened by the sights about her Susan was too obsessed to quit until she had seen the last dead man. If Sardo was not among them there was a chance one or more of the others might be. It would narrow her hunt, but she preferred all four men alive so she could personally gun-shoot them and enjoy their slow, agonising deaths. She moved to a body near the bushes, toed it over onto its back and instantly paled in recognition as she stared down at the face, untouched by buzzards.

Even in slack-jawed death the black-stubbled features were brutal. An old bullet scar, deeply gouged beneath the left cheekbone, ran along the side of his face. The dark, glazed eyes seemed to leer at her as they had in the flickering lamplight of her parents' ranch house.

Susan trembled at the frightening memory, and others it brought in rapid succession, then was overcome by impotent rage. There was no earthly revenge she could extract. A bullet through the heart had brought a quick death instead of the lingering one she had planned. All she could do was spit contemptuously into the corpse's face and stalk away, leaving it exposed for the buzzards.

A slight rustle of bushes halted her in mid-step. Susan twirled, glimpsed a gaunt, shaggy-bearded face looking back at her through the tangled branches, and mentally chided herself for leaving her rifle in the saddle holster.

But the hard-eyed stranger had a rifle — and it was aimed straight at her.

A cry trapped in her throat, Susan stood stock-still and stared, wide-eyed, into the face of new death.

8

Winchester in hand, Rhone swung from the saddle and studied the footprints around the rear of the buckboard. The floured tracks crossed straight over the others and moved to the edge of the hollow. They were deeper, the man evidently carrying provisions, and the turned up dirt and tuffs of grass were recent, too recent for comfort.

'Climb down slow and easy,' Rhone said softly, not looking at Brad and appearing to be engrossed in the other tracks. 'Keep your horse between you and that end of the clearing on your right.'

Brad had been in Rhone's company long enough to obey without question. Striving for casualness, he pretended to tighten the strap on a saddlebag pocket. 'You believe we are being watched?' he asked quietly, raising his eyes to peer over his saddle.

'There's a damn good chance,' Rhone answered. 'Where's Susan?' He half-turned, looked over his shoulder and muttered disgustedly, 'Now what's she doin'?'

Brad followed Rhone's gaze and saw Susan standing like a statue near the edge of the clearing, staring intently at something beyond the bushes. Whatever it was must be very important to have diverted her from her task. He was about to remark upon that to Rhone but did not have the chance.

'You two by the waggon,' a gruff voice shouted from the bushes, 'don't try nothing or the girl takes a bullet.'

'He has a rifle, Rhone,' Susan called uneasily.

A great wave of fear for Susan's safety swept over Rhone. He quickly measured the exposed distance to the edge of the clearing. It was too far to chance — and even if he made it, the man would surely drop Susan before giving him his full attention. 'You a

Dagget,' he called, playing for time, 'or one of Sardo's men?'

'Neither. How about you?'

'Sardo's got somethin' we want.'

'He killed my family,' Susan said coldly.

'So you see we got no call to fight,' Rhone called, his amiable tone belying his tension.

'We ain't — as long as the girl fetches me her horse.'

'Then what?' Rhone asked.

'I ride outta here, and you can go square accounts with that bastard Sardo.'

'Sounds like you two have done more than just 'howdied'?'

'We have,' came the bitter reply.

'Then you'd know where to find him, wouldn't you?'

'I might — but first I'll have that horse. Bring 'im here, girl, and remember this rifle will be on you the whole time.'

As Susan, her reluctance plain, turned and slowly started for her horse directly across the clearing, weaving around or stepping over a dead man, Brad whispered to Rhone, 'Why doesn't he take one of our horses?'

'Can't. It would mean havin' to change positions, and he couldn't keep Susan or us in his sights while he's movin'.'

'Once he has a horse he has no reason to tell us a thing.'

'He's not leavin' here with it,' Rhone said flatly. Watching Susan's progress, he continued, 'When I give the word you git your horse around the other side of this buckboard and keep him there.'

Susan reached her grazing horse, took the reins and started back across the hollow. The horse caught the smell of blood and death and panicked, snorting and rearing, desperately trying to pull away. Avoiding the thrashing hoofs, Susan clung to the reins and spoke soothingly. Thoroughly spooked, the horse refused to heed and continued backing away, towing her along as she vainly dug her bare heels into the ground. The animal reared again, forelegs climbing the air, and Susan allowed the reins to be torn from her hands. The horse wheeled and plunged into the woods. Susan dove after it and rolled behind the shelter of a broad tree trunk.

'Now!' Rhone said to Brad, and they hastily led their mounts around the far side of the buckboard.

From his concealment Ed Kobeck cursed his lost chance as he saw the blonde and her horse were lost to him. Dammit, he should have figured the horse would raise a ruckus at being led across that clearing. He swung his Henry repeater toward the two men but was too late. A futile shot kicked splinters from the top side of the buckboard and its resounding report set the circling buzzards to screeching. Sweating despite the early morning, he sombrely debated what he would do next.

'Looks like you're plumb outta luck,

friend,' Rhone called while he and Brad tied their reins to the rear wheel. He threw a random shot, high, in the direction of the rifle smoke drifting from the woods.

'We need him alive,' Brad cautioned.

'He will be,' Rhone said. 'That was just to show him we ain't afraid to shoot back.' He turned and called to the opposite side of the hollow. 'Susan, stay put and keep outta this, hear?'

'I hear,' she replied sourly over the squawking birds.

Hoping she would indeed do as she had been told, Rhone turned back and shouted, 'Awright, friend, we can still bargain. Hold your fire and listen good.'

'I'm listening,' the voice called, a little nearer then before.

'We got a big stake in findin' Sardo. Help us do just that and you'll be paid right handsome.'

'Fifteen hundred dollars,' Brad put in. 'But you must take us to him.'

'Not on your life!'

'I am prepared to pay more — only if you guide us directly to Sardo.'

'Don't trust me, huh?'

'Why should we?'

'I say we'll find him without you,' Rhone called, 'it'll just take longer. My partner's rich and likes to give money away. If you're smart you'll take some of it. Git us to Sardo, and you're free to ride on and not share in the fightin'. Now make up your mind and quit wastin' our time. I got better things to do than killin' you.' He slowly and deliberately levered a fresh round into the Winchester's chamber, the sound of the action sharp and clear, emphasising his determination to continue the fight if need be.

For a time only the grating, incessant carrion birds were heard above, adding to the growing tension, then the man's voice grumbled crossly, 'Double the amount — and I cut as soon as we're in sight of the place.'

'Agreed,' Brad stated firmly.

'Show yourself and we'll do the

same,' Rhone called and began edging around the rear of the waggon.

Bushes rustled and a gaunt, big-boned man in torn work clothes cautiously emerged. His black scruffy hair and beard almost obscured his sun-darkened features. Rifle under one arm, he dragged a bulging, rattling gunny sack of supplies after him. He was a far cry from what Rhone and Brad expected, and they stood staring dumbfounded at the approaching near skeleton who appeared to have just risen up from amongst the littered dead.

* * *

Leaving the clearing to the buzzards, who had gathered in greater numbers, the four halted to rest and eat on the other side of one of the two hills. The smell of death still lingered in the others' nostrils and almost cut the gaminess of their new companion. Gorging himself like a famine wolf, Ed Kobeck fended off anxious questions with grunts and incoherent, food-spewing words until his stomach was finally content, then insisted on first relating his tale. Brad and Susan stewed, sympathetic, but impatient to hear about their own concerns; still they left the handling of Kobeck up to Rhone, who listened with true interest. When the time was right Rhone brought the subject around to the Dagget massacre.

Begrudgingly shifting his coarse, admiring gaze from Susan, Kobeck addressed Brad. 'If your woman was that redhead Sardo took off, then she's destined to become Nelson Forbes' new woman till he tires of her. When that happens she'll be given to his guards . . . ' He broke off with a shrug.

Brad made to speak, but Susan leaned forward and quickly interrupted. 'Then Sardo must have come to my father's ranch on Nelson Forbes' orders. My father suspected the existence of a slave mine in the area, and had written the Territorial authorities.'

'I wouldn't put it past him,' Kobeck agreed, using the opportunity to again direct his gaze to Susan.

'And he got no place with his letters?' Rhone asked.

'Now the reason is plain,' Susan said. 'Nelson Forbes is one of the richest and most influential men in the Territory.' Her eyes glittered with hate. 'The only sure justice is to kill him.'

'That's a sure enough fact,' Kobeck said and nodded his shaggy head. 'Now who's going to do it?'

'Whoever gits to him first,' Rhone said, dead-flat.

'That's no easy matter,' Kobeck said. 'You'll see when you get there.'

'Nothin' in life is ever easy,' Rhone said, his face a mask of unconcern.

'Are you forgetting about Lorna?' Brad asked, alarmed.

'We probably won't git in and out without some shootin',' Rhone replied soberly, 'so we might as well see to it that the right folks git shot while we're there.'

'I am going to kill Sardo and Forbes,' Susan said stonily.

'You can all draw straws and shoot whoever you want,' Kobeck interjected. 'But my deal is to lead you there — nothing more.'

'Nobody's askin' you to take a hand in this,' Rhone said. 'But you've sure got reason to, if you're of a mind?'

'I'm not,' Kobeck said firmly.

'Then suppose you start earnin' your keep,' Rhone said, his tone conveying it was an order rather than a suggestion, 'and let's git on the trail.'

'It's your party,' Kobeck said. He swigged down the last of his coffee and stood. 'The sooner this is done,' he commented gruffly, 'the better I'll like it.' A glance at the sombre faces about him showed that he spoke for all.

9

Sardo and the remnants of his small army rode along the crest of a towering ridge. Beneath them the green, pine-clad slopes dropped away like the spreading skirt of a splendid gown, and occasionally they could make out the hairline that was the distant trail over which they had travelled. The grandeur went unnoticed by all, even their captive.

To Lorna Miller mountain riding was absolutely fear-inspiring. Before, lying bound in the Dagget buckboard, she had mercifully been spared the sight of the treacherous trails. Now she was sitting astride a horse, ankles tied to the stirrups and wrists affixed to the saddle horn, clinging with white knuckles, and able to see her surroundings. The one-eyed man led her horse by its reins, and she could only put her trust in him and her animal's sure-footedness. A slip would spell disaster, as she would be carried over the edge of the trail with her horse.

Resisting the gnawing, perverse temptation to lean sideways and peer down (for she now most firmly believed the stories of great heights luring persons to their deaths), Lorna forced herself to keep her eyes either focused on Sardo's back or the distant mountain peaks. In an attempt to divert her mind she once more pondered her new situation.

Except for being kept tied, she had so far been treated with a crude courtesy. Her questions about her intended fate had gone unanswered by Sardo, and she was left wondering about this Mister Forbes. As no law-abiding citizen would send a man like Sardo to an outlaw town to purchase a woman at a slave auction, he was, therefore, disreputable. Hopefully, he was of a higher calibre than the Daggets, but that certainly would not take much.

Again Brad came to mind and Lorna's eyes misted. She must believe that he somehow had survived the desert and was searching for her. Logic rejected it, but could not totally extinguish the flame of hope. And she knew she must cling to hope (no matter how small) if she was to endure whatever hardships lay ahead.

* * *

After nooning in a canyon clearing, with pine forests behind them, Rhone and his group had pushed on into a narrow, rock-strewn pass. Minds and bodies dulled by lack of sleep, they allowed their mounts to pick their way along the trail. There was mutually no thought of surrendering to exhaustion; besides the possibility of overtaking Sardo before he reached the mine, they were goaded by nature. Since late morning grey clouds had begun forming and slowly closing in on the mountain, rumbling intermittently as they swooped lower, blown by a growing wind that threatened to hasten the inevitable downpour.

'Mountain weather is tricky,' Kobeck commented, seated behind Brad. 'Just like a woman, you can never count on it to stay good-natured too long — especially this time of year.' He threw a bright-eyed look over at Susan who chose to aloofly ignore him and not be drawn into undesired conversation.

'It'll hold a spell longer,' Rhone said, eyeing the darkening clouds. 'Leastways till we're outta this pass. Then everybody better start keepin' an eye out for a good shelter.'

After over half an hour of silent climbing they emerged into a broad clearing, fringed with giant pines and young aspen. They were almost across the open area when the sky finally opened up and let loose its deluge. Rain roared down in hard, wind-driven sheets, drenching the riders and glistening on their animals' sleek coats while turning the bare earth into soggy, slithering mud. Head bent against its pelting sting, Rhone led the mad, slippery charge into the timber, and reined up beneath the arching branches on a thick, brown carpet of pine needles.

'We can't stay here,' Kobeck said, peering up at the sky through the dripping branches. 'These tall trees draw lightning, like flies to molasses.' As if confirming his words great streaks of lightning played across the dark sky followed by deafening booms of thunder.

Rhone looked to Susan who, shivering, teeth involuntarily chattering, sat her horse, uncomfortably aware that her wet shirt was enticingly moulded against her tall, graceful body. Before she could misinterpret his gaze, he turned, dug into his bedroll and pulled out a patched, well-worn, yellow slicker. 'It's a mite late,' he said somewhat sheepishly and offered it to her.

Brushing her plastered hair back from her face, Susan smiled and said gratefully, 'It is still welcome.' She quickly slipped on the crackling, oversized slicker and fumbled with its large buttons.

Aided by sporadic flashes of lightning, they penetrated deeper, ducking beneath frequent low branches, and presently found themselves staring across a short, open area at a sheer, towering rock wall. A lightning display lit the sky like day, revealing a bisecting, wide-mouthed cave through the hazy, grey veil of rain.

'That's what we're looking for,' Kobeck said eagerly.

They rode to the cave, grouped the horses under a granite overhang that shelved the entrance, and hauled their gear inside. The interior was large, deep and high-ceilinged. Thankful for the dryness, they stretched out wearily on the hard-packed dirt floor. But in a few minutes Susan was up and gathering dry sticks and wood lying beneath the rocky overhang and inside the cave's mouth. The men roused themselves to help her, and soon a fire was crackling, its illuminating flames banishing the coldness and throwing dancing shadows on the walls and ceiling. Hands outstretched, they huddled nearer the fire's toasty warmth.

'Surely you don't intend to sit around in those wet clothes until they dry?' Susan enquired. Keeping a straight face at their clear consternation, she added, 'You will all catch pneumonia and be no good to yourselves or anyone else.'

Modest glances were passed, then Rhone shrugged. 'The lady's right, gents.' He began unbuttoning his clinging shirt. Brad and Kobeck hesitantly followed suit.

'Honestly, you are worse than a bunch of old maids,' Susan said in mock disgust. She rose and announced, 'I'll gather more wood. Call when you are decent.' She turned and, rustling slicker swishing about her ankles, walked out through the mouth of the cave.

All eyes followed her out and held for a moment, to be certain she had disappeared into the darkness, then the men exchanged glances. 'Let's git to it and not keep her waitin' out in the cold,' Rhone said and hastily stripped off his shirt.

Outside Susan, keeping a modest eye on the cave entrance, quickly used the opportunity to shuck the slicker and remove her soaked shirt. Cringing with a gasp as a sudden gust of wind-lashed rain slapped her naked body, she crammed the shirt part way into one of the pockets and again donned the slicker. After fastening every button, she set herself to the task of collecting firewood. By the time she had a respectable armful, Rhone's voice invited her back into the cave.

Susan entered and almost burst out laughing at the sight of the three men, blankets about their waists, sitting around the fire like pale-skinned Indians; all that was missing was a peace pipe. But the thought of how ludicrous she must look herself swathed from neck to ankles in the large, shapeless slicker stilled any comment. Clutching his blanket, Rhone started to rise to help her. Susan shook her head, dumped the wood on top of the pile and took her place at the fire. She pulled out her shirt and held it up to dry.

The fire was kept blazing while the clothes dried; conversation was sparse, awkward and mostly meaningless. When the clothes were dry enough, the fire was allowed to die down for cooking and the 'wood-gathering' ritual was repeated. Shirt on beneath her slicker, Susan returned with less wood than before and found the men dressed and in better spirits. Depositing the wood, she removed the slicker, which was uncomfortable in the cave's warmth, and helped Rhone with the cooking. Thanks to Kobeck's sack of supplies they enjoyed a decent, filling meal that night. Food and warmth took swift toll and the four fell asleep in their blankets around the fire.

Later Ed Kobeck awoke, eyes heavy with sleep. From his place near one wall he peered across the flickering light of the dying fire at Susan Prescott, moaning and twisting in a troubled sleep. Well, she wasn't the only one. It was a desire to escape his own dreams, more than the girl's sounds, that had awakened him. He lay listening to the steady rain and silently cursing his luck. For all of his thirty-three years good fortune had eluded him, no matter what he had turned his hand to.

A series of business failures (some quite shady) had sent him West from Ohio with high hopes of cashing in on the gold and silver in Colorado. Instead, broke and lost, he had been found stumbling about in the wilderness by one of Nelson Forbes' periodic patrols. He had found gold all right, but it was completely useless to him.

The memory of those brutal years were etched as permanent nightmares in his mind — and he was running the risk of returning to that hell. If only the girl's horse had not panicked he would be down the other side of the mountain by now and on his way to safety. Another time three thousand dollars would have seemed a fortune; now it was small recompense for the danger involved.

Kobeck lay there stewing. The only smart thing to do would be to steal one of the horses and leave while the three were still sleeping. The rain would cover his trail. Chances were they would not waste time tracking him but continue on in search of Sardo. Easing himself up on a forearm, he cast a furtive glance about the sleeping figures beyond the dwindling fire. The girl and the dude were no threat, only Rhone. It would be an easy matter to remove that threat right now. His hand slipped toward the holstered six-gun and gunbelt coiled beside him.

Susan moaned and stirred again, her sleep becoming more fitful. Yanking his hand away from the gun butt, Kobeck's eyes jumped to her. She did not awaken. As he continued tensely watching her, there suddenly came the harsh realisation that the killing could not stop with Rhone. He must kill everyone if he wished to completely ensure avoiding the hangman's noose. Damning one and all, he struggled with his latest quandary.

Minutes marched by on stumped legs. Outside the rain sluiced down as the storm, with its accompanying thunder and lightning displays, showed no intention of letting up any time soon. It seemed to reflect Kobeck's mood, especially when he puzzlingly found that he was not the animal he imagined he had become. The cold-blooded murders of a sleeping woman and two men was utterly abhorrent. The only course open was to slip out quietly without tangling with Rhone and ride as fast and as far as he could.

His mind set, Ed Kobeck cautiously began to put his plan into action.

10

Thrashing and whimpering, Susan Prescott was deep in the relentless grip of a recurring nightmare. Eyes squeezed tightly shut, she urgently willed herself to awake, but the terrifying images only continued to vividly play across her mind's eye. All she could do was allow the now-familiar dream to run its dreaded course . . .

★ ★ ★

Spurs. Jingling, flashing in the fluttering lamplight. Men's distorted shadows gliding across the walls and ceiling. The stench of splashing whisky and kerosene.

She was no longer on her bed, but stretched out on the floor in the front room where the bodies of her parents and older brother were sprawled in dark pools of their own blood. She was also utterly helpless, her ankles now tied as well as her wrists, on which she lay. It was the coolest time, the hours just before dawn, and her naked body was taut with cold from head to toe as the night air invaded the room through the open front door. Her pain-throbbing cheek brought vile memories of the four men's individual faces, ending with a brutal blow by the man with the painted eyepatch while she had lain tied and sobbing on her bed. She was confused by the needless act of cruelty and why she had been moved in here.

Suddenly all became clear as the flickering lamp flew across the room and smashed in a far corner. The men ran to their waiting horses as smoke and flames, fanned by the outside breeze, flared about the room and ran up the walls to the ceiling.

Her head lifted quickly as racing hoofbeats receded into the night. She was alone — left, supposedly unconscious, to die inside the burning house. She could not lie there. In only scant minutes, seconds, the flames would be upon her. She must somehow find a way to free herself.

Desperation rampant within her, she turned onto a hip, removing her body weight from her arms. The movement sent shocks of pain through her wrists and ankles. Rows of rope gouged her flesh as she struggled, twisting fingers failing to reach the harshly-tied knots. Smoke and heat stung her eyes, threatening to clog her throat and nostrils, as the steadily-moving flames lanced toward her helpless form like reaching, inhuman fingers.

Abandoning her useless efforts, she frantically thrust herself away from the advancing inferno. Her smarting eyes teared, obscuring her vision, as thick smoke engulfed her. Guided only by the cool air, she hitched her way, crablike, toward the open door. Progress was slow. Ropes bruised her wrists and ankles. Her body glistened wetly from exertion and the intense heat as other high flames spread, eating everything they touched.

One wall became a sheet of flames. Deprived of its support a fiery, overhead beam wavered, then crashed down with a mad swirl of hot embers. The roaring flames deafening her ears, she agonisingly pulled herself across the floor. It was difficult to feel anything but searing heat.

Then, hacking and fighting for breath, she was in the doorway.

An urgent kick of her long legs sent her out into the cool, fresh night air, stubbornly pursued by a billowing cloud of grey-black smoke. She coughed smoke from her raw lungs and exhaustedly gulped in the untainted air. But the crackling flames reminded her that she was not yet out of danger; she still needed to be safely clear of the blazing house before it collapsed.

At the further expense of her bruised and torn wrists and ankles, she laboriously rolled her body over and over on the uneven ground and came to rest, belly-down, a dozen yards away. She lay waiting for her self-imposed agonies to diminish, and shivered as the cold gradually settled into every nerve and fibre of her overheated body.

There was a sudden explosion of glass quickly followed by another. Starting, she squirmed onto her side and shook the clinging, dishevelled hair back from her wet face.

Dense smoke and tongues of fire licked out through the front door and the now broken windows on either side. The whole house was aflame.

Tears blurred her eyes. She was watching the death of the life she had known. From this night on everything had changed. Nothing would ever be the same again. She drew her knees up to her body and lowered her head. In a moment she was sobbing, softly at first, then great racking sobs shook her body. Her head jerked up as the house groaned like a living thing in pain.

The roof swayed, screeching timbers

cracking, and abruptly collapsed with a thunderous crash, burying the bodies of her family under mounds of flaming debris. Embers danced like bright fireflies. Smoke and flames chased them high into the dark sky.

Then came another sound: strange, awful, soul-rending — and she realised she was screaming . . .

* * *

Susan burst to the surface of sleep's dark pool with a panicked cry lodged in her throat. A hand was on her shoulder. She opened her eyes wide and saw a shadowy form looming above her. Shaking her head wildly, she gasped and recoiled, clawing for the rifle beside her.

'Whoa now, you been dreamin',' Rhone said calmly. 'And none too good by the sound of things.' He released her shoulder and leaned back, the dying fire lighting his concerned face.

Susan relaxed and sat up, flushing and lowering her eyes. 'It wasn't . . . ' she said in a small voice and shuddered at the memory. She laced her slender fingers together and stared down at them self-consciously while composing herself. Attempting to hide her vulnerability, she looked up and said coolly, 'I'm sorry I disturbed you.'

'Nothin' to be sorry for,' Rhone said and gave an easy shrug. 'We all have 'em from time to time. It's only natural.' Her expression softened and he added, 'I've sure had more than my share.'

Surprise briefly flickered over Susan's face at his admission, then was replaced by scepticism. 'Please don't treat me like a child.'

'I ain't,' Rhone said sincerely. 'I'm tryin' to be helpful.' He saw her confusion and pressed on. 'Just remember, no matter how bad they seem, they're only dreams and that's all.' Susan gave a small nod and again looked down at her hands in her lap.

'Care to talk about it? Sometimes that's best.'

Susan shook her head. 'It's gone now.' After a pensive moment she asked, 'You are being nice . . . why?'

'It don't cost nothin',' Rhone answered with evasive casualness. He saw her slightly tense and quickly spoke before she could revert into her familiar sullen shell. 'And maybe because I like you.'

Susan's head jerked up. 'You have an odd way of showing it,' she said disbelievingly. 'Until now, all you have done is argue — and knock me unconscious and tie me up.'

Now it was Rhone's turn to momentarily flush. 'Well, you ain't exactly been a 'bright, little ray of sunshine' yourself.' Guilt lent an unintentional edge to his light tone.

Their eyes met stubbornly, but the truth of the other's words held tempers in check. Susan was the first to relent and break the strained silence. 'I suppose neither of us has been the best of company . . . '

Rhone was more than ready to seize the compromise. 'That's all in the past . . . if you'll let it be?'

Susan made a pretence of considering, then shrugged and smiled hesitantly. He grinned warmly, and she permitted herself a complete smile. Both were suddenly aware of their nearness as they sat, silent, motionless, gazing into each other's eyes. A strange, consuming force blanketed them. For that moment, as though by mutual, unspoken agreement, they lowered their previous defences and allowed their looks to convey the loneliness and need in their secret, inner selves. Susan's head tilted back slightly, longlashed eyes half closed in unconscious anticipation. Slowly, almost imperceptibly, Rhone's head bent towards hers. But then the special moment was lost.

In the darkness beyond the mouth of the cave the horses whinnied and shifted about nervously; apparently something other than the storm was agitating them.

Instantly drawing away, Rhone wasted no time in finding the source. His ranging eyes settled on Kobeck's empty place. Then he was on his feet and dashing from thé cave, unaware of the confusion on Susan's face as disappointment briefly swelled inside her. Quickly grasping the situation, she threw off her blanket, shouted to Brad, then snatched her rifle and ran after Rhone.

Brad groggily sat up, rubbed his sleep-slick eyes, and saw Susan disappear outside. He was alone in the cave, and from the commotion over the driving rain something was happening. Gathering his rifle and gunbelt, he stumbled off to join the others.

Outside Brad almost collided into Susan who stood watching, clutching but not raising her rifle, as Rhone grappled to pull Ed Kobeck from his rearing horse. Hindered by the other two shrilling and stamping horses and Rhone's tall horse balking at a strange rider, Kobeck was unable to force the animal from the sheltering rock overhang and out into the pouring rain. Brad fidgeted, uncertain whether to aid Rhone, and threw a questioning look to Susan who was too engrossed to notice. Then the problem was solved as Rhone, taking an overhanded fist on one shoulder, jerked Kobeck from the horse's slick, bare back by the gunbelt, and they fell to the ground on their sides.

Despite the soggy earth, the wind was driven from Kobeck in a huge grunt. Still, he fought instantly, attempting to ram a savage knee up into Rhone's groin. Rhone quickly rolled away from the incapacitating blow. They came to their feet almost simultaneously and lunged, swinging with both fists. Rhone smashed Kobeck in his bearded face, but he closed on him. They slipped and went down, locked in each other's arms. Gouging, slugging and kicking, they rolled out into the pelting rain.

'Shouldn't we stop them?' Brad asked Susan.

'We will,' Susan said calmly, 'when the time is right. They have to get the anger out of their systems first.'

The men struggled to their knees, hammering blindly and futilely at each other in the rain and darkness. Kobeck began to weaken under the deadly mauling of Rhone's more accurate fists as bone crunched against bone. Then he was flat on his back in the mud, bloody and beaten, with Rhone straddling his chest, still slugging powerful, sledging blows that snapped his head sharply from side to side.

Susan nodded to Brad and ran to the edge of the overhang. 'Rhone, that's enough,' she shouted over the wind-driven rain.

'Yes. You'll kill him,' Brad seconded.

Rhone paused and, sucking in deep gulps of air, looked over at them. 'That's what happens to horse thieves — and he's tried it twice now!'

'We still need him to find the mine,' Brad countered.

'He's served his purpose. We got

the name, and we can find it without him.'

'There are other things he can tell us,' Susan said.

The rain had restored Kobeck's dazed senses and he fully grasped his precarious position. 'Y . . . you don't know the lay out,' he said desperately. 'I can show you — and you'll need a diversion when you go in there.'

'You said you wouldn't go anywhere near that place,' Rhone reminded him harshly.

'I've changed my mind,' Kobeck said hollowly.

'And you'll change it again when we git there.'

'I won't,' Kobeck said and shook his head vehemently, large eyes bulging out of his bearded face. 'I give you my word!'

'The word of a horse thief?'

'Please listen to him, Rhone,' Susan implored.

Talk had cooled some of the rage that had flared within him during the fight, but it was the thought of looking small in Susan's eyes by killing a defeated man that tipped the scales in Kobeck's favour. The man was well cowed at the moment — but how long would he stay that way? Rhone felt Brad and Susan's anxious eyes on him and reluctantly made his decision.

'All right, for now,' he relented. He saw the tension start to drain from Kobeck's face, grabbed his shirt front and raised his head, thrusting his face close to his. 'You go back on your word,' he said in a quiet, deadly voice that only they could hear over the heavy rain, 'and I'll kill you.' He saw Kobeck's tension return and added, 'That's a promise I fully intend to keep.' He let Kobeck's head drop back into the mud, then slowly stood, lingering to turn his face up to the rain for a calming moment, and staggered back under the overhang to Brad and Susan.

'I'll go build up the fire,' Susan said, eyeing his sodden appearance.

'Fine,' Rhone said. 'I'll be in directly.' With that he moved off to tend his horse, now huddled with the others against the wind.

Making a bid to arouse some sympathetic response, Ed Kobeck groaned loudly and laboriously sat up. When neither Brad nor Susan made a move to help him, he clambered to his feet and slogged forward under his own steam.

Susan shivered from the cold and the uncontrolled brutality she had witnessed. It was expected of Kobeck, but not of Rhone, who had finally revealed to her a gentler side of his nature. She hated Kobeck for spoiling that moment and plunging her back into the grim world she had briefly forgotten. She stonily turned as Kobeck came up and hurried back inside the cave; Brad followed, leaving the bedraggled man to straggle after them.

Rhone replaced the horse's hobbles and made to leave. His mind was clearer now, and it occurred to him that Kobeck's escape try had been for the best. Before, he would have left them within sight of the mine. But now he was obligated to stay and guide them in, making the job a whole lot simpler. No time would be wasted in aimless searching. Kobeck knew right where to go, and the safest way to get there. He had also been right about the need of a diversion; exactly what it was would be decided when they arrived. At the moment Kobeck was intimidated, and Rhone planned to see he stayed that way until this mess was over.

The wind lashed drops of stinging rain under the rock shelf, rousing Rhone from his thoughts and sharply reminding him of his chilled state. His mind a trifle easier, he tramped toward the cave and the welcome warmth of Susan Prescott's waiting fire.

11

The morning was bright and clear, with no hint of the previous night's storm. Early morning rays filtered through the pines as the four left the clearing and climbed toward the summit. The violence of the night had taken its toll, and a sullen atmosphere doggedly surrounded them. Talk had been nil on leaving the cave, and there was still no inclination to break the silence when they reached the summit at mid-morning and paused to dismount and breathe the horses. The heavy rain had washed away any tracks, and they were left to wonder if Sardo's party had also been stalled on the mountain.

Wishing for a pair of binoculars, Rhone stood staring down the winding, tree-lined trail and its switchbacks. There was no movement of any kind as far as the eye could see. Before they had started out Kobeck, still smarting from his beating, had sourly informed him that once they were down the mountain it was less than half a day's ride to Nelson Forbes' valley. It would take well past noon to get down the mountain, so chances were pretty slim that they would catch up with Sardo before he reached the valley. All they could do was push on at their best pace (which wasn't all that fast with Kobeck switching riding double with him and Brad, as Susan flatly refused to allow him near her) and stick to the original plan.

Rhone turned back to his party. Susan, face pensive, paced restlessly beside her horse while Brad and Kobeck lounged against a large rock on the edge of the trail. Not much of an army to go up against a nest of professional gunmen. Of course he wasn't planning a head-on cavalry charge, but a game of stealth: in and out with the least possible fuss. All three had deep grudges, and that made them more determined than any gunhawks who fought solely for money.

Contenting himself with that reasoning, Rhone gave an order to mount and walked to his horse. The three wordlessly obeyed, Kobeck climbing up behind Brad, and Rhone led the way down the trail.

★ ★ ★

Slender fingers of her bound hands wound together around the pommel, Lorna rode slumped forward, half-dozing in spite of the jolting pace. They were out into open country and well away from the rolling foothills where they had camped last night in the scattered timber, after completing a harrowing descent from the mountain in the driving rain. She was once more following behind Sardo's erect figure, a rope running from her horse's neck to his saddle horn, as he rapidly led the way toward a group of distant mountains.

Above the sun neared its zenith, spreading a heat that, for the time, was a pleasant contrast to the chill of the utterly miserable night. Still, it could not dispel the cold Lorna felt inside at the thought of what fate awaited her in the mountains ahead. She again tried (almost successfully this time) to convince herself that Brad was in pursuit with a well-armed constabulary. That did not seem impossible, as long as she refused to dwell on the exact details of how it had been accomplished. Well, she was too weary to think anyway.

Making her mind a blissful void, Lorna resumed dozing and ignored the brooding, ever-nearing mountains.

★ ★ ★

When word came that Sardo had been spied approaching the valley with a woman in his company, Nelson Forbes had been sorely tempted to ride out to meet him on the trail. However, an adherence to propriety held him in check. One never went to a hireling, but let the person come to him. And he certainly had no wish to appear an eager suitor in the woman's eyes. She would get fanciful notions soon enough. It never failed. No matter how meek the woman when she arrived, in time constant familiarity fostered a delusion of self-assured possessiveness (as it had with Rosa and those before her) that inevitably led to her removal, as swiftly as a replacement could be found. He had no illusions that this woman was any different, but she would be something new to enjoy while it lasted.

The ledger opened before him on his large desk was too tedious to hold his attention so Forbes settled back in his padded swivel chair and smoked a cheroot to idly pass the time. Rosa was upstairs taking her *siesta* and there was no sense waking her with the bad news until after he had approved the new arrival. It would be a mere formality, as Sardo had long ago proven to be as good a judge with women as he was with horses.

Forbes had just crushed out the remains of his cigar when hoofbeats approached the house. Moments later Manuelita, the plump Mexican housekeeper, appeared in the open doorway and confirmed Sardo's arrival. Forbes gave orders that he and the woman were to be shown in and to gather several servant girls outside the study. The housekeeper withdrew, and Forbes fastidiously brushed lint and stray ashes from his dark coat while he waited. Presently heavy, jingling footsteps and the slapping of bare feet came along the hall. Forbes straightened in his chair and assumed his usual air of casual superiority.

Thrusting a bedraggled young woman ahead of him by one arm, Sardo entered the room. 'She don't look all that much now,' he announced cheerfully and steered the stumbling redhead toward the desk. 'But wash the trail dust off, put her in clean duds, and you'll be more'n proud to claim her.'

Forbes ran a critical eye over the weary woman as she stood rubbing her rope-bruised wrists and staring back at him with cool green eyes. In spite of her dishevelment and filthy rags her beauty was plainly evident. He nodded in agreement and addressed her, 'What is your name?'

'*Mrs* Lorna Miller,' Lorna answered aloofly.

'I see,' Forbes said, unimpressed. Her thick Yankee accent grated upon his Southern ear. 'And where is your husband?'

'We were separated when I was abducted by our guide and taken to Free Town.'

'I took her from Pa Dagget,' Sardo put in.

'My husband's family is wealthy,' Lorna said evenly. 'They will pay handsomely for my safe return.'

'I am sure they will,' Forbes said

patiently. 'Unfortunately, I already have far too much money to care.' He saw her disappointment and added pleasantly, 'You will adjust much better to life here if you think of yourself as a widow.'

'I prefer to regard myself as what I am: a married woman who is your prisoner.'

'As you wish,' Forbes said patronisingly. He looked past Lorna to the doorway as sandalled footsteps and a small group of low Spanish voices were heard in the hall. He called Manuelita inside and motioned to Lorna. 'Take the lady to one of the guest rooms for the time being and see that she is made presentable to join me for dinner.'

'I have no appetite.'

'Then you may watch me dine.'

'I fear I will be indisposed,' Lorna said and touched the back of a hand to her brow.

'Dinner will be at eight,' Forbes said smoothly. 'Manuelita will escort you to the dining room.' He saw her face cloud and pressed on before she could speak. 'Please do not make me have to fetch you. I do so dislike physical exertion right before dinner.'

The veiled threat was well understood, but Lorna carefully kept her face impassive. Summoning what dignity she could, she turned, walked to Manuelita and was ushered out into the hall where three young, giggling servant girls were waiting to escort her upstairs.

'She has spirit,' Sardo commented dryly, listening to the woman's fading sounds. 'Maybe a mite too much.'

'One must never confuse spirit with obstinacy,' Forbes said casually. He indicated a chair before the desk and opened a box of cigars for Sardo. 'Now tell me about Pa Dagget. Did he suffer?'

* * *

Sardo had concluded his report and left with glowing praise and a promise of an extra bonus, when the angry clicking of French heels in the hall abruptly reminded Forbes of a chore left undone. He looked up from his papers as Rosa stormed into the room, short skirt swirling.

'Nelson, who is that *gringa* upstairs?' she demanded stridently, her voice strung with excitement and a measure of concern.

Forbes rose from his chair and moved around the desk to meet her as she stalked up. Her raven hair was matted and her venomous face was puffy with sleep, emphasising the dark circles beneath her flashing eyes. Forbes now saw only a harridan instead of a beautiful woman. 'I should think you would have already guessed,' he answered blandly.

'I wish you to tell me,' she shrilled unpleasantly.

'It is quite simple,' Forbes said, his voice deceptively casual. 'She is your replacement. Now gather your belongings and take them to the women's quarters. You may keep whatever trinkets I have given you.'

A flicker of surprise went over Rosa's face, showing that she plainly did not believe him, then the rage returned. 'No. I am your woman.'

'You were bought in Free Town with my money,' Forbes agreed without raising his voice. 'Therefore, I may do with you as I please. You no longer amuse me, but perhaps you will amuse the guards?'

'The guards!' Rosa echoed.

'That is my usual procedure. Surely you knew from the start, or were you naive enough to think it would never happen to you?'

'But I love you.' Unfortunately, a hint of desperation spoilt the desired sincerity, and disproved Forbes' cynical belief that all women were expert liars.

'You love your position of being my mistress.'

Rosa shook her head emphatically. *'Mi amor,* I can still make you love me, too. I possess more passion than any fair-skinned *gringa.'* She took a step toward him, another, then was stopped abruptly by Forbes' hard, arrogant smile.

'Please do not prolong this unpleasantness. It is over, Rosa, so run along like the little lady you always wanted to be.'

Rosa's eyes flashed fire, her body trembled from the outrage she felt. Shrieking, she flung her skirt up, snatched a stiletto from its thigh sheath and came at him with the grace of a cat.

Forbes easily caught her upraised wrist and disarmed her with a twisting wrench, sending the knife clattering onto the desk. Her free hand swiped at his eyes with sharp nails. He jerked his head away and knocked her to the floor with a backhanded sweep. Restraining his impulse to do more, Forbes stood sombrely eyeing Rosa who lay sobbing miserably.

'P . . . please . . . *mi amor* . . . I did not mean to hurt you,' Rosa managed between thick sobs. 'I *love* you . . . do not sent me away . . . '

'Perhaps I acted in haste,' Forbes said quietly, apparently moved by her words. Still groggy from the blow, she raised her head and squinted up at him. 'I will not give you to the guards.' He smiled reassuringly and extended his arms to her.

Tears glistening down her cheeks, Rosa stood and hurried forward with no hesitation. *'Mi amor . . .'* she cried joyously, flinging her arms around his neck and thrusting herself against him. She crushed her eager lips on his in a fiery kiss of passion.

Forbes responded, felt her relax in his arms, then let one hand slip away and locate the stiletto on the desk. Still holding the kiss, he viciously drove the slender blade up under Rosa's rib cage to the hilt. She reared with a whimpering gasp and stared up at him in pain and disbelief. Her quivering lips tried to form words, but she could only shake her head sadly. A glitter of hard satisfaction in his dark eyes, Forbes withdrew the knife with a twist and stepped back as Rosa crumpled to the floor. Her eyes were glazing, filled with the agony preceding death, and he had only a moment for her to hear him.

'You see, Rosa,' Forbes said softly, 'I did not give you to the guards after all.'

12

All day they had relentlessly pushed their horses in a desperate race against the westbound sun. Thanks to a short cut shown by Kobeck, they were now staring down at a wide valley whose sides rose in timbered tiers. The sun had almost set, only its upper rim showing above the mountain ringing the valley's far side. Pink streaks stretched across the sky, coating the bellies of clouds. The mountain's massive shadow was spreading to engulf the entire valley, bringing a faint coolness to the air. While there was still light Kobeck quickly identified each of the cluster of shacks situated well away from the huge main house and its sprawling grounds.

'The workmen,' Rhone drawled, eyeing a long weathered building not far from several yawning mine shafts, 'they got the gumption to fight, or are they bunch of jack rabbits?'

'Every one of them hates Forbes' guts, but they can't go against the guards without guns.'

'We'll see to that,' Rhone said, switching his gaze to the weapons and dynamite shed Kobeck had pointed out previously.

'Win or lose, they'll provide the diversion you need,' Kobeck said, pleased with the plan.

'*We* need,' Rhone reminded him. 'Or are you fixin' to change your mind again?' His set, unrelenting face made the bearded man shake his head resignedly.

'Suppose Kobeck is wrong and the workers will not fight?' Susan asked, attempting to clear the tension and steer the talk back to the business at hand.

'If revenge ain't good enough for them,' Rhone said, his piercing eyes remaining on Kobeck, 'there's also his gold.' As he expected, a glow of renewed interest came over Kobeck's face.

'It is only fair,' Brad added. 'They certainly have every right to it.'

'Damn straight,' Kobeck said thickly, his eyes roving the mine shafts. 'I worked and sweated for years, and I have a right to all the gold I can pack — and then some!'

'You'll git that chance tonight,' Rhone said evenly. It was a waste of breath, Kobeck's mind was already filled with thoughts of a life of luxury, at long last. Rhone turned to the others. 'Nothin' we can do now but wait till full dark.' He walked back toward the tethered horses. Brad went after him, leaving Susan to watch the activity below with Kobeck, who was preoccupied with his own thoughts.

Rhone was loosening his horse's cinch strap, letting the saddle-girth sag, when Brad walked up. 'Rhone . . . ' he began.

'Best make your horse comfortable, too. We're gonna be here a long spell.'

He pulled his Winchester from its saddle holster. 'New moon this night. Make sure you ain't wearin' anythin' bright, or it'll shine like a mirror.' He hunkered down and began rubbing dirt over the length of the rifle barrel.

Brad kneeled, wiped dirt over his silver buckle, then followed Rhone's example with his two Colts. 'Are you certain this 'diversion' isn't going to place Lorna in further jeopardy?'

'Not as long as we git to the main house first.'

'But Forbes . . . '

'He don't know we're after her,' Rhone interrupted. 'He'll think it's a workers' uprisin' and send most of the guards around the house off to help quell it.' He laid the Winchester aside and took out his six-gun for the same treatment. 'You're overlookin' the fact that you got a better chance of gittin' shot than her.'

'I know,' Brad said soberly. 'And if that happens I depend on you to see that Lorna returns safely to Boston.'

'I'll see to it you *both* git safely to San Francisco, if you still wantta go there?'

'We do.'

'Then stick close to me when the trouble starts, and do whatever I say.' They stood and leathered their revolvers. 'I'll take care of your horse,' Rhone said. 'How about sendin' Susan here and keepin' an eye on Kobeck? We don't want him goin' off after that gold ahead of us.'

'He won't,' Brad said, and walked away.

Leaving his rifle on the ground, Rhone moved to the other horses. He had just finished uncinching both animals when he turned to see Susan entering the tiny clearing.

'Brad said you wanted to see me?' she said, moving to him.

'I been thinkin',' Rhone said, choosing his words carefully. 'Now that we got a whole army of workmen to back us, there's no sense in you goin' along.'

Susan stared at him in complete

surprise. Then she shook her head in confusion and said in a slow, hurt voice, 'You wanted my help when we first met . . . and in Free Town, too.'

Rhone nodded. 'But that was before . . . '

'Before what?' Susan demanded, her big eyes suddenly blazing at him.

'Before I started caring about you,' Rhone answered, keeping his voice level. 'I don't want anythin' to happen now.'

Susan's exquisite face softened into a warm smile. 'I don't want anything to happen to either of us,' she said, sincerely touched. She took a deep sighing breath that lifted her bosom beneath her calico shirt and kept her steady gaze upon Rhone. 'The killers of my family are down there, and if I do not go I will never have a moment's peace.'

Rhone stared back at her, his mouth a tight, hard line. 'I know all about revenge, and what it can do to you.' Susan frowned questioningly, all of her attention fully directed on him. 'I was married after I got back from the War. She waited four years, while I was off with Hood's Cavalry. Two months later she was dead, murdered by three jayhawkers who were hidin' out in the Big Thicket.'

'Rhone, I am so very sorry,' Susan said gently.

'Were the men ever found?'

'I tracked them down in the swamps and left the 'gators feedin' on all three of 'em.' Rhone looked away from her and stared off reflectively. 'After that I became a bounty hunter, and kept on killin' till I was all burned out inside. Got to where I didn't care about myself or anybody.'

'Yes . . . I know . . . ' Susan said sadly, her voice scarcely above a whisper, and touched his arm.

Rhone turned back to her. 'Finally I quit — more'n a year now — and tried my hand at prospectin'.' He smiled wryly. 'Didn't quite work out. But after this business is done tonight I'll have enough to buy a ranch and settle down . . . ' He abruptly took her shoulders and firmly drew her to him. 'Damn it, Susan, I don't want to lose you, too!' She made no effort to pull away as he kissed her fervently. Her tall, supple form moulded against his granite contours and they clung together as if this first kiss might be their last.

Slowly, with great reluctance, Susan disengaged herself from Rhone's embrace. 'Please, Rhone . . . don't ask me to stay behind. I will do anything else — but not that.'

'I could keep you here . . . '

'You could,' Susan agreed, her tone becoming as cold as a blue norther. 'And I would hate you for it the rest of my life.' She held herself straight and unyielding.

The intent of her words was unmistakable and Rhone struggled with the conflict surging inside him. He reminded himself that Susan had acquitted herself well so far — and she sure had pulled his bacon out of the fire during his fight with Templeton. It would mean he'd have to keep an eye on both her and Brad in the upcoming fracas; but he had an idea Brad would take more looking after than Susan. Rhone let out a heavy breath, his frustration draining out with that simple act and leaving him oddly relaxed. 'Well, I guess you'll do to take along,' Rhone said dryly. A smile played at the corners of Susan's mouth and slowly became genuine. Rhone walked to his rifle and picked it up. 'This Winchester shoots faster than your old Spencer.'

'Won't you need it?' Susan asked, moving before him.

Rhone shook his head and placed the rifle into her timidly outstretched hand. 'It'll be more of a hindrance. My pistol will be fine for close work.'

'Thank you, Rhone,' Susan said and tucked the rifle under her arm.

'You know, the world wouldn't stop turnin' if you was to call me 'Phil'?'

Susan blushed sheepishly, lowered her eyes briefly, then held him with her steady gaze and gently reached out to touch his face with her forefinger. 'All right . . . Phil,' she said in a low, sultry purr that sent a delightful tingle up and down the length of Rhone's backbone.

'That didn't hurt much, did it?' Rhone said happily. Susan shook her head and smiled, her moist lips parting. She was close enough so that her pale, disarrayed hair gave off a delicate feminine scent that tantalised his nostrils. Rhone slid an arm around her tiny waist and drew her to him, gently this time. She reached up with her free hand, pulled his head toward hers and kissed him tenderly. But before the kiss could become too serious she pushed him away with a trembling hand, her breath caught in her throat. Rhone wasn't breathing quite right himself.

'We should go back to the others,'

Susan said, her voice breathy with emotion.

'Yeah,' Rhone agreed glumly and turned to leave. He took a step and hesitated as he felt Susan's hand on his shoulder. He turned to see her beside him, smiling warmly, her large eyes twinkling. He smiled back at her, draped an arm around her slim shoulders, and she snuggled against him, her arm slipping around his waist.

Together they walked from the clearing.

13

The four waited until dark to make their way to the floor of the valley, where they crouched in the shadowy brush and again surveyed the area while waiting for a pack of slow-drifting clouds to obscure the full moon. Lights glowed in most of the windows of the distant main house, as well as in its back yard. The nearer guards' shacks and those of the women also showed lights, and small groups of rowdy men came and went. Set away from the other buildings, the workers' barracks were dark.

'When we go,' Rhone said, glancing to the others, 'take off and don't stop runnin' till you git there.'

'But that is well over a hundred yards . . . ' Brad began.

'Nearer two hundred,' Kobeck cut in.

'Suppose the cloud cover does not last?' Susan asked, finishing Brad's question.

'Indians learned a long time ago that at night one long unbroken movement draws less attention than a bunch of stops and starts,' Rhone replied. 'Nobody knows we're around so they got no call to be watchin' for us.'

The flock of clouds finally began moving aimlessly across the face of the moon, and the four were up and running through the darkness. Luck was with them and they only had to cover the last fifteen yards in the moonlight. Lungs threatening to burst, they pressed against the side of the long shadowy building and waited for their breathing to return to normal. Snores and a few muffled voices reached them from inside the windowless structure. Rhone drew his Colt and cautiously led the way along the weathered building. Reaching the corner, he cautiously peered around, pistol ready.

A lone guard, his brutal features briefly lit by the glow of a cigarette, was slouched on a bench with a shotgun beside him. His attention was more on the laughter and rowdiness coming from the women's quarters than on anything else.

Reversing his hold on the Colt, Rhone stole forward. The guard caught his slight sounds and started to turn, hand grabbing for the scattergun. Rhone put his full weight behind the blow, the pistol butt catching the man in the vulnerable spot right behind the ear and cracking his skull. He caught the dead body by a thick shoulder and propped it back against the wall. He beckoned to the others, moved to the door and took down a key ring hanging on a large nail. As the three joined him, he focused his attention on Kobeck.

'You know those men inside so you talk first. Tell'em the plan — and make it short and sweet.' Kobeck nodded and took the key from him. While Kobeck fumbled to insert the key into the heavy padlock, Rhone glanced to Brad. 'You and Susan keep watch. We won't be long.' Kobeck dropped the open lock to the ground and went inside with Rhone.

Brad and Susan backed into what shadows they could find and stood tensely staring toward the various shacks as the workers' building suddenly became alive with activity. The noise quieted as quickly as it has started and was replaced by low, droning voices. The wait seemed for ever, but was actually only several minutes. Rhone stepped out, followed by Kobeck and two equally filthy and ill-clad men. One man eagerly snatched the guard's shotgun while the other quickly relieved the dead man of his gunbelt and six-gun.

'Me and these two are goin' to the weapons' shed,' Rhone informed Brad and Susan. 'When I signal send the men out in groups of twelve. Anythin' goes wrong, cut and run for the horses with Kobeck.' He turned and moved off with the men before Brad or Susan could respond.

Their movements helped by scudding clouds, the three crossed the thirty yards to the large shed. The shotgun's heavy butt shattered the lock, and Rhone and the men entered, closing the door behind them. Rhone struck a match, located a lantern on a nail on a post and lit it, turning the wick low in case any light escaped through cracks in the walls.

'There's enough here for a whole army,' he remarked, eyeing the boxes of rifles, shotguns and cartridges.

'The dynamite is stored here, too,' said the man with the shotgun, 'so be careful with that lamp.'

'Start opening them crates,' Rhone said, handing the lantern to the other man, 'while I signal for the men to join us.' He went out, carefully shutting the door so no light would escape from inside, then took off his hat and waved as he stepped out into the moonlight. Kobeck waved back, and Rhone withdrew from the light. Drawing his pistol, he stood ready to give covering fire as the first group of men started out of the workers' building.

The men crossed without incident and hurried inside the shed. Rhone caught the last man's arm. 'A couple of you come back out and stand guard; the rest stay inside till everybody's here.' The man grunted and trailed in after the others. Rhone turned and watched for the next group to start across.

★ ★ ★

Promptly at eight o'clock Lorna, elegantly attired in an evening gown that bared her slender shoulders and more of her bosom than she preferred, was shown into the dining room by Manuelita, who discreetly withdrew and closed the door. Nelson Forbes greeted her with all the charm of a Southern cavalier, but she ignored him and took her place at one end of the long table. A Mexican girl served them and then left Lorna alone with Forbes.

Having eaten only dry hardtack and several strips of tough venison jerky since morning, Lorna's stomach reminded her that resolutions were made to be broken and she begrudgingly surrendered to the tempting meal before her. Forbes was gentlemanly enough not to gloat.

Dinner was eaten in near silence, except for several unsuccessful attempts at pleasantries by Forbes. Forbes pushed his empty plate aside and leaned his elbows on the table as he watched Lorna finish. She primly folded her hands in her lap and looked across at Forbes' smiling face.

'Now may I kindly return to my room, sir?' she asked, trying to make her voice casual.

'Wouldn't you care for a glass of champagne?' he enquired. 'I thought we might have it out in the garden.'

'I wish to retire,' Lorna said, her

voice unintentionally sounding small and tight.

'I desire the 'pleasure' of your company a while longer.' Forbes gave her a slow, twisted smile as he stood and moved toward her. Lorna pushed back her chair and made to rise, but he slammed an open palm on the table, rattling the dishes and candelabras. 'You will remain seated, madam.' Lorna's eyes opened wide and she held herself rigid. Forbes stopped beside her and reached down to stroke her bare shoulder. 'I have tolerated your petty disposition long enough. You are here — and here you will stay until I decide otherwise.'

'I have nothing but the utmost contempt for you,' Lorna said, glancing up at him, hands clasped tightly in her lap. 'Time will not change my feelings.'

'I care nothing about your feelings,' Forbes said, his eyes glittering with wicked amusement. Lorna said nothing. He gave an unpleasant laugh, then yanked her up from the chair by her arm and his right arm encircled her waist, locking her against him.

'Let go of me,' Lorna cried furiously, but the arm clamped around her did not budge as she tried to rip herself away from him. Forbes' mouth muffled any further outcry. Lorna whimpered and twisted in his arms. She wrenched her mouth from his and struggled violently, their movements upsetting the chair.

It hit the floor unheard, for at that same instant a jarring explosion echoed through the valley.

The struggling couple momentarily froze, startled and confused, clinging to each other for support as the whole house shook. No sooner had the sound died than gunfire laid its harsh echoes over the valley. Forbes shoved Lorna away and made for the door; she tripped over the chair and went down in an unladylike tangle of legs and petticoats. Forbes ignored her and bolted from the room.

'What the hell is going on here?' he bellowed at two guards charging toward him down the long hallway. The panicked shrieks of servant girls came from various parts of the house and added to the confusion as another deafening charge obscured the men's replies. Hand braced against a wall, Forbes moved to meet the men.

'Workers somehow got loose, Mister Forbes,' the first man answered.

'They got hold of the dynamite and are blowin' hell outta everythin'!' the second man put in, quite unnecessarily.

'My new woman is in the dining room,' Forbes said, gesturing back down the hall. 'Protect her, and also see that she does not try to escape.'

'Sure thing,' said the first man.

Before the men could leave Forbes added, his voice utterly cold, 'Should anything happen to her, neither of you better be alive to tell me.' They nodded uneasily and started off, and Forbes rushed to his den to arm himself from his array of weapons.

Three guards were gathered on the veranda when Forbes stalked out, shotgun in hand, six-guns dangling from both hips and another tucked into his belt. The fighting was coming nearer, still at peak intensity. Limned in the pale light of the full moon distant figures could be seen surging back and forth, red, orange, and yellow flashes of their various weapons and the accompanying sounds gave the impression of watching a fireworks display.

'Where is Sardo?' Forbes barked, sending the men whirling to face him.

'Guess he's out there somewhere,' answered the tallest man. 'If he's still alive, that is.'

Forbes intently studied the chaotic battle and slowly began to make out some semblance of order. The retreat was not a complete rout, some were waging a rearguard action. That meant that Sardo, a former military man, was alive and supervising the withdrawal. The attack stalled. The guards drew nearer, spreading out to flank the main house, where Sardo apparently intended to make a stand. A sudden explosion blew a gaping hole in the ranks of the rearguard, hurling earth and ghastly debris in all directions, and the dazed survivors were overwhelmed by the charging workmen. Then the retreat did indeed turn into wild disorder, but the attackers were hindered by the thick smoke from the explosion and the multitude of discharging weapons.

'We have seen enough,' Forbes grimly announced as the fast-approaching battle neared the immaculate lawn. 'Go inside and take up positions at the windows.' The three guards needed no further prompting. Forbes delayed to see that Sardo's iron will had restored some order, then strode inside and slammed and locked the front door. Unfortunately, there was no way to lock out the impending battle into which he would be thrust as a most unwilling participant.

14

Hollering and shooting, Rhone and the others pursued the fleeing guards across the lawn and up to the well-lit main house. There the badly outnumbered guards turned to make a stand, some taking shelter behind the white columns. Spurred on by hatred and killing-lust, the workers fell upon them in a wild rush before Sardo could effectively organise firing ranks. Though Rhone had kept Brad and Susan with him since the beginning, he now lost sight of both in the swirl of bodies and acrid gunsmoke as the battle became a series of small contests.

Susan caught sight of Sardo backing to the front door and, nimbly avoiding two men locked in hand to hand combat, ran up the steps to the veranda. A brawny workman shoved ahead of her and was shot down by the one-eyed man. Finding the door locked, Sardo pounded on it, then turned as Susan screamed his name at the top of her lungs to be heard over the commotion.

Sardo hesitated, surprised to see a woman in the midst of the fighting — then came recognition, disbelief, and a swift realisation of danger. He started to raise his lowered Colt.

Susan shot him flush in the chest.

Face contorting, Sardo slammed back against the door as a searing pain expanded inside his chest. He knew he was a dead man — but he was not about to die alone. This time he would finish the job on Prescott's blonde daughter. His one good eye was blurring as his trembling hand struggled to raise the suddenly heavy six-gun while there was still a breath of life left within him.

Susan quickly levered the Winchester and yanked the trigger. The hammer fell with an ominous click. She desperately tried again. The rifle was empty. Sardo's Colt was up, about to train its still smoking muzzle on her.

Then Susan was roughly shoved aside, colliding against a bullet-scarred column, and another six-gun barked twice in rapid succession.

Shoulder shattered, Sardo's arm abruptly fell, his aborted shot gouging a hail of splinters from the veranda, and his body reeled sideways in a macabre, haywire dance as the second bullet drove through the side of his skull. Leaving a wide, red smear, he collapsed lifelessly on one side of the door.

Susan whirled and saw Rhone, smoking Colt in hand, grinning at her. 'That makes us sorta even now,' he said dryly. Before she could respond they were jostled aside by a group of men who stormed the front door, battering it with their shoulders. Rhone made his way back to Susan, firmly took her arm, then pulled her down the steps and off to one side.

'Rhone!' Susan protested, wrenching her arm free from his grip.

'You got Sardo,' Rhone snapped, 'so stay outta the rest of this.'

'Forbes is still alive!'

The front door crashed open, sagging on its broken hinges, and Forbes, in shirtsleeves, stood planted in the foyer, shotgun ready. It bucked with a thunderous roar and a deadly hailstorm of sizzling buckshot cleared the doorway of intruders. Discarding the empty scattergun, Forbes drew both six-guns and backed away, firing, as other men clambered over the bodies of the dead and writhing, shrieking wounded. Those attackers met the same fate. Six-guns empty, Forbes took the one from his belt and ran into a room off the hall.

'That coulda been you up there,' Rhone said sternly.

'And just as well *you*,' Susan shot back. She gave a startled squeal as Rhone shoved down forcefully on her shoulder and simultaneously hooked a boot behind her ankle and tripped her to the ground. Long legs spraddled, she landed none too gently on her pert backside.

'Now stay there,' Rhone growled and moved to the steps, leaving Susan fuming and rubbing her aching buttocks. He heard Brad's call and turned to see him rush up, both Colts in hand.

'We must get into that house and find Lorna,' Brad said breathlessly.

'That's what we're gonna do,' Rhone said calmly. 'Stay behind me and keep your eyes open.' He led the way up the steps, past the sprawled bodies and cautiously inside the house.

Glancing about her, Susan saw that the fighting was now isolated on the sides of the house. Then she heard men on the veranda and tensed as an angry voice cried Forbes' name. Rapid shots were traded through a large broken window and two workmen buckled and went down. She saw Kobeck fire into the room from one side of the window, then curse and smash away the remaining shards with the barrel of his six-gun. Susan leaped to her feet and dashed up the steps as Kobeck climbed through the window. She paused to snatch one of the dead workmen's pistols, then went climbing in after Kobeck.

Carefully minding the broken glass, Susan pussyfooted away from the window where one of Forbes' men lay face down in his own blood. She begrudged the delay, but crippling her bare feet in haste would end any pursuit. Gunshots racketted from an adjoining room, followed by two sets of heavy, running footsteps. Safely away from the glass, Susan broke into a run.

Out in the long hall Rhone and Brad heard the gunshots in another part of the house and tensely paused. Suddenly two men, guns drawn, stepped out of a room farther down the hall. Rhone fired without delay and Brad followed suit with both Colts. One man dropped without firing a shot; the second man's shot sent the derby spiralling from Brad's head. Then he was slammed back against the doorframe by a storm of slugs and, pistol firing aimlessly, collapsed inside the room. A woman's terrified scream quickly filled the momentary silence.

'Lorna!' Brad cried and ran forward ahead of Rhone.

'Slow down, you don't know for sure,' Rhone shouted, but was ignored. Gunshots still boomed from the other side of the hall, now apparently from rooms near the back of the house. Rhone paid no heed and headed after Brad. He caught him as he reached the doorway and flung him back against the wall. 'Hold it, or you might git your head blown off,' he cautioned sharply. 'Let me go in first.' He ducked into a crouch and stepped into the room.

While Brad waited impatiently a tall man burst from a room near the end of the hall, moved to the back door and, flinging it open wide, went out. Cussing and yelling Forbes' name, Kobeck came charging out of the room and straight through the open doorway with Susan Prescott hard on his heels, and it dawned on Brad that he had just glimpsed the infamous Nelson Forbes.

'C'mon in here, Brad, and lay claim to your wife,' Rhonc called cheerfully.

All other thoughts vanishing, Brad holstered his twin Colts and rushed inside to see Lorna, hair and elegant gown mussed, standing by the dining table with Rhone. For several heartbeats all they could do was stare, as though fearful that if either spoke or moved the other would vanish. Then with a joyous half gasp, half sob, Lorna was in his arms and they clung together fiercely, speaking their love.

Isolated gunshots took Rhone's attention from the happy couple and reminded him of a chore left undone. 'Just take it easy in here till it's all over but the shoutin',' he said and turned toward the door. 'I'm gonna find Forbes.'

Abruptly remembering, Brad jerked

away from Lorna. 'He's in the back yard. Kobeck and Susan went after him.'

'Susan?' Rhone said in surprise.

Brad nodded and started to speak, but Rhone urgently bolted out the door. He turned to Lorna and began to explain away her confusion.

* * *

The decorative Japanese lanterns gave off a festive glow that was in dire contrast to Rhone's dark concerns as he ran through the back yard, following the retreating gunshots which came from beyond the small group of shacks where women's voices were heard wailing and praying in Spanish. Reaching the end of the shacks, Rhone saw a barn and corral about fifty yards ahead. Kobeck and Susan were closing in when a spurt of flame lanced out of the dark barn doorway, the fiery muzzle blast briefly revealing a man's figure, and Kobeck went down in a heavy somersaulting fall. Susan returned fire then quickly sought shelter behind a corral post. Shouting her name, Rhone started forward.

Rhone was almost to Susan when a barebacked rider abruptly burst from the barn. She stepped out into the open, fired at the man clinging to the horse's neck, and the animal broke stride and crashed to the ground, a bullet through its skull. The man flung himself from the animal's back, rolled to his knees and fired. With a cry, Susan slammed back against the corral rails and limply slid to the ground.

Rage and haste caused Rhone's shot to miss, but it turned Forbes from the direction of the barn and sent him racing off into the darkness when his own pistol clicked empty. Rhone let him go and went directly to Susan, passing Kobeck whose unnatural position left no doubt as to his fate.

Kneeling, Rhone set down his Colt and gently raised Susan up into his arms. There was blood in the hairline of one temple, but the movement of her uplifted bosom showed she was breathing. Rhone eased back the mass of yellow hair and was relieved to see the bullet had only grazed her, knocking her unconscious. He expelled his tight breath in a long oral sigh and hugged her to him. Then he heard his name and looked around to see Brad and Lorna approaching from the area of the shacks.

Damn, didn't *anyone* mind what he said?

Still, Rhone was glad to see them. 'He don't need no help,' Rhone called as the two neared Kobeck and slowed, 'but Susan does.' He carefully lay Susan down, picked up his revolver and stood.

'Is she badly hurt?' Brad enquired, coming up with Lorna.

'Just knocked cold,' Rhone replied. 'See to her while I finish with Forbes.'

'I am going with you,' Brad said.

Rhone shook his head and replied

grimly, 'This is somethin' personal — between him and me.'

Brad did not argue, but watched Rhone jog away, then kneeled to help Lorna minister to Susan.

15

Rhone caught up with Forbes near the foot of a mountain when his headlong flight almost spilled him into the 'death pit'. He triggered his Colt as Forbes fumbled shells into his empty weapon. The round misfired. Incapable of further thought in his lust for revenge, Rhone dropped his gun and barrelled into Forbes before he could sight his revolver. Discharging into the air, the six-gun leaped from Forbes' hand as the men smashed to the ground.

They tossed about in a violent heap, battering each other with both fists. Their struggle took them to the very edge of the pit, where they swayed and then plunged over. Rhone managed to disengage himself from Forbes during the fall and avoided being pinned beneath him as they crashed down.

Shaken by the harsh impact, both men lay motionless and groaning. In near unison they shook off their grogginess and gained their feet, backing away and warily circling while still recovering. Forbes abruptly rushed with both fists cocked and they stood toe to toe, their explosive gasps and involuntary grunts merging with the meaty percussion of fists on flesh.

Forbes missed with a hard right that Rhone ducked under, then winced and stumbled back as a fist ploughed into his belly. Rhone pressed after him, swinging both fists, but Forbes' tottering form was in motion and instinctively rolled with the blows. Rhone set himself for another punch, threw it at Forbes' jaw, and missed as he continued to back away. Forbes saw his chance and took it, pitching forward and clubbing a fist against the side of Rhone's neck. The brutal force rocked Rhone and he fell to one knee, his head sagging.

Quickly stepping up close, Forbes

clasped his hands together and, raising them high above his head, hammered them down at Rhone's face. Rhone found the strength to jerk his head forward right before the blow could land, and Forbes was wrenched off balance. Before he could right himself, Rhone lunged, drove his head into his stomach, and they both went down in the dirt. Wretching for air, Forbes desperately threw Rhone from him as he tried to straddle him and rolled away. Forbes dragged himself to his knees and hesitated as a glinting object caught his eye.

It was one of the two pickaxes that had been left in the pit from the last workers' combat.

Forbes scrambled up and made for the pickaxes. Rhone was not in time to stop him. Forbes grabbed the weapon and whirled, facing Rhone and placing himself as a barrier to the other pickaxe a few feet away. His looping swings struck only air, but effectively thwarted Rhone.

Weaving and ducking, Rhone was relentlessly forced to give back under Forbes' wild assault. Too late he realised that Forbes' seemingly rash attack was coolly calculated, and he was being herded back against a dirt wall. Rhone feinted a lunge to the left but went to the right. Forbes was not taken in. Rhone felt a savage rush of air as he leaped back, narrowly avoiding a slash that would have ripped his belly open from hip to hip, and slammed into the dirt wall.

Face contorting into a cruel grin, Forbes raised the pickaxe and came in for the kill. At the last instant Rhone hurled himself to the side and the point sank deeply into the wall. Before Forbes could wrest the weapon free Rhone was on him, smashing with both fists and knocking him away from the impaled pickaxe. Forbes fought back viciously, driving with his knee and fists, and slowly worked his way back to the handle.

As Forbes started to grab the pickaxe,

Rhone caught his shoulder and whirled him around. His right fist flattened Forbes' nose and his left crashed into his jaw. The effort to keep his balance, with arms outflung, left Forbes wide open. Rhone ploughed in, knuckles smashing Forbes' blood-smeared face and hurtling him backwards.

A cry of pure agony burst from Forbes as he fell heavily against the other sharp end of the pickaxe and was impaled. His large, shocked eyes stared down in bewilderment at the bloody point protruding from the centre of his chest, further marring his once-white dress shirt. Then his body spasmed and hung limply against the wall.

Rhone took a last sober look, then turned and walked away. As he wearily scrambled up out of the pit he was anxiously met by Brad, Lorna and Susan, who wore a strip torn from Lorna's white petticoat as a bandage about her forehead. Before he had a chance to speak, Susan flung her long, willowy body into his arms.

'Phil . . . thank heavens you're all right,' she cried, and began covering his face with kisses.

'How about you?' he enquired.

'Just an awful headache,' Susan answered, then ended further conversation by pressing her lips to his.

* * *

Late morning found the four sitting their horses and watching as groups of former workmen straggled out of the valley with their spoils.

'I feel rather guilty about taking a share of Forbes' gold,' Brad said, patting his saddlebags.

'Why?' Rhone asked. 'He inconvenienced you and Lorna, didn't he?'

'He certainly did,' Lorna replied.

'Just look at it this way,' Rhone said. 'If you was ever to git tired of bankin' you got the means to do somethin' else.'

'Such as joining you and Susan in cattle-ranching?' Brad said.

'Ain't a bad life,' Rhone said and shrugged. 'There's some lean years at first, but that don't matter — if you got the right person workin' alongside you.' He turned and grinned over at Susan, who smiled back at him.

'Perhaps some day we'll consider that?' Brad said.

'You do that,' Rhone said easily. 'But right now we got a ride ahead of us to that stage station.'

Futures bright, the four rode from the silent valley and put the past behind them . . .

THE END

Other titles in the Linford Western Library

THE CROOKED SHERIFF
John Dyson

Black Pete Bowen quit Texas with a burning hatred of men who try to take the law into their own hands. But he discovers that things aren't much different in the silver mountains of Arizona.

THEY'LL HANG BILLY FOR SURE:
Larry & Stretch
Marshall Grover

Billy Reese, the West's most notorious desperado, was to stand trial. From all compass points came the curious and the greedy, the riff-raff of the frontier. Suddenly, a crazed killer was on the loose — but the Texas Trouble-Shooters were there, girding their loins for action.

RIDERS OF RIFLE RANGE
Wade Hamilton

Veterinarian Jeff Jones did not like open warfare — but it was there on Scrub Pine grass. When he diagnosed a sick bull on the Endicott ranch as having the contagious blackleg disease, he got involved in the warfare — whether he liked it or not!

BEAR PAW
Nevada Carter

Austin Dailey traded two cows to a pair of Indians for a bay horse, which subsequently disappeared. Tracks led to a secret hideout of fugitive Indians — and cattle thieves. Indians and stockmen co-operated against the rustlers. But it was Pale Woman who acted as interpreter between her people and the rangemen.

THE WEST WITCH
Lance Howard

Detective Quinton Hilcrest journeys west, seeking the Black Hood Bandits' lost fortune. Within hours of arriving in Hags Bend, he is fighting for his life, ensnared with a beautiful outcast the town claims is a witch! Can he save the young woman from the angry mob?

GUNS OF THE PONY EXPRESS
T. M. Dolan

Rich Zennor joined the Pony Express venture at the start, as second-in-command to tough Denning Hartman. But Zennor had the problems of Hartman believing that they had crossed trails in the past, and the fact that he was strongly attached to Hartman's Indian girl, Conchita.

BLACK JO OF THE PECOS
Jeff Blaine

Nobody knew where Black Josephine Callard came from or whither she returned. Deputy U.S. Marshal Frank Haggard would have to exercise all his cunning and ability to stay alive before he could defeat her highly successful gang and solve the mystery.

RIDE FOR YOUR LIFE
Johnny Mack Bride

They rode west, hoping for a new start. Then they met another broken-down casualty of war, and he had a plan that might deliver them from despair. But the only men who would attempt it would be the truly brave — or the desperate. They were both.

THE NIGHTHAWK
Charles Burnham

While John Baxter sat looking at the ruin that arsonists had made of his log house, a stranger rode into the yard. Baxter and Walt Showalter partnered up and re-built the house. But when it was dynamited, they struck back — and all hell broke loose.

MAVERICK PREACHER
M. Duggan

Clay Purnell was hopeful that his posting to Capra would be peaceable enough. However, on his very first day in town he rode into trouble. Although loath to use his .45, Clay found he had little choice — and his likeness to a notorious bank robber didn't help either!

SIXGUN SHOWDOWN
Art Flynn
After years as a lawman elsewhere, Dan Herrick returned to his old Arizona stamping ground to find that nesters were being driven from their homesteads by ruthless ranchers. Before putting away his gun once and for all, Dan forced a bloody and decisive showdown.

RIDE LIKE THE DEVIL!
Sam Gort
Ben Trunch arrived back on the Big T only to find that land-grabbing was in progress. He confronted Luke Fletcher, saloon-keeper and town boss, with what was happening, and was immediately forced to ride for his life. But he got the chance to put it all right in the end.

SLOW WOLF AND DAN FOX:
Larry & Stretch
Marshall Grover

The deck was stacked against an innocent man. Larry Valentine played detective, and his investigation propelled the Texas Trouble-Shooters into a gun-blazing fight to the finish.

BRANAGAN'S LAW
Alan Irwin

To Angus Flint, the valley was his domain and he didn't want any new settlers. But Texas Ranger Jim Branagan had other ideas. Could he put an end to Flint's tyranny for good?

THE DEVIL RODE A PINTO
Bret Rey

When a settler is cut to ribbons in a frenzied attack, Texas Ranger Sam Buck learns that the killer is Rufus Berry, known as The Devil. Sam stiffens his resolve to kill or capture Berry and break up his gang.

THE DEATH MAN
Lee F. Gregson

The hardest of men went in fear of Ford, the bounty hunter, who had earned the name 'The Death Man'. Yet even Ford was not infallible — when he killed the wrong man, he found that he was being sought himself by the feared Frank Ambler.

LEAD LANGUAGE
Gene Tuttle

After Blaze Colton and Ricky Rawlings have delivered a train load of cows from Arizona to San Francisco, they become involved in a load of trouble and find themselves on the run!

A DOLLAR FROM THE STAGE
Bill Morrison

Young saddle-tramp Len Finch stumbled into a web of murder, lawlessness, intrigue and evil ambition. In the end, he put his life on the line for the folks that he cared about.

BRAND 2: HARDCASE
Neil Hunter

When Ben Wyatt and his gang hold up the bank in Adobe, Wyatt is captured. Judge Rice asks Jason Brand, an ex-U.S. Marshal, to take up the silver star. Wyatt is in the cells, his men close by, and Brand is the only man to get Adobe out of real trouble . . .

THE GUNMAN AND THE ACTRESS
Chap O'Keefe

To be paid a heap of money just for protecting a fancy French actress and her troupe of players didn't seem that difficult — but Joshua Dillard hadn't banked on the charms of the actress, and the fact that someone didn't want him even to reach the town . . .